A Slow Smile Spread Across Her Face. "Well, Well, This Is An Interesting Situation," She Said.

"It'll be cleared up in a few months. But meanwhile..." Zach shrugged helplessly.

"Meanwhile, someone has to run this place. And you did just fire me...." she said.

"Not in so many words. I'll hire you back. I'll double your salary! But you don't want to leave, anyway," he said with certainty. "So what do you want, Ellie? You want me to grovel?"

She pretended to consider this. "That has a certain appeal. But no, there's only one thing that will keep me here. One little condition."

"And that is?" He dreaded her next words.

"You have to stay here and work with me."

Dear Reader,

Another year is drawing to a close here at Silhouette Desire, and I think it's a wonderful time for me to thank all of you—the readers—for your loyalty to Silhouette Desire throughout the years. Many of you write letters, letters that we try to answer, telling us all about how much you like the Desire books. Believe me, I appreciate all of the kind words, because let's be honest . . . without *you,* there wouldn't be any *us!*

In the upcoming year we have many sexy, exciting stories planned for you. *Man of the Month* is continuing with books by authors such as Diana Palmer, Joan Hohl, Ann Major and Dixie Browning. Ann Major's SOMETHING WILD series is continuing, as is Joan Hohl's BIG BAD WOLFE series. We will have special "months of men," and also duets from authors such as Raye Morgan and Suzanne Simms. And that's just part of the Desire plan for '94!

This month, look for a wonderful *Man of the Month* title from BJ James. It's called *Another Time, Another Place,* and it's a continuation of her stories about the McLachlan brothers. Don't miss it!

So once again, thank you, each and every one of you, the readers, for making Silhouette Desire the great success that it is.

Happy holidays from

Lucia Macro
Senior Editor . . . and the rest of us at Silhouette Desire!

KAREN
LEABO
FEATHERS AND LACE

SILHOUETTE *Desire*®
Published by Silhouette Books
America's Publisher of Contemporary Romance

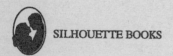 SILHOUETTE BOOKS

ISBN 0-373-05824-1

FEATHERS AND LACE

Copyright © 1993 by Karen Leabo

Printed in U.S.A.

KAREN LEABO

credits her fourth-grade teacher with initially spark-
ing her interest in creative writing. She was determined at an early age to have her work published.
When she was in the eighth grade, she wrote a children's book and convinced her school yearbook publisher to put it in print.

Karen was born and raised in Dallas. She has worked
as a magazine art director, a free-lance writer and a
textbook editor, but now she keeps herself busy full-
time writing about romance.

One

_____

Was *that* supposed to be an airport? From two thousand feet up, Zach Shaner peered down skeptically at the minuscule strip of asphalt, then checked his navigation chart. There could be no mistake. This had to be the Rocky Ridge Airfield.

It wasn't the danger of landing that bothered him. He'd landed the small Piper Cub in tighter spots. It was what the tiny "airport" symbolized that irritated the hell out of him. He was about to touch down in the boonies.

There was nothing wrong with life in the country, he supposed, so long as he wasn't the one living it. He didn't enjoy interrupting a very busy work schedule to fly to this remote corner of Oklahoma, but the longer he put it off, the worse this problem was going to get.

If he had to inherit a ranch, why couldn't he inherit one right outside a big city?

For the next couple of minutes, Zach concentrated on the tricky landing, easing back the throttle with a practiced hand, watching the ground rise to meet him. When the plane touched down he quickly braked to a smooth stop. Piece of cake. Thank goodness he owned a plane and knew how to fly it. Otherwise he might have spent days just *getting* here. He taxied off the runway onto the grass and cut the engine.

The airport was deserted, he noted, as he vaulted to the ground. The only sign of civilization, a squat, brick building with a faded sign reading Tornado Air Freight, appeared to be locked up tight. There definitely was no sign of the woman he'd talked to on the phone, Ellie Kessler, who was supposed to escort him to the Red Canyon Ranch.

Though he hated the whole idea of this trip, he was at least looking forward to meeting Ellie. She had a Southern drawl, spoken in a low, honeyed voice that made him think of whispers in the night. Would her face and body match that voice?

Probably not, he conceded, as he retrieved his luggage from the back of the plane. Most likely she was a sturdy farm girl wearing overalls, work boots, and sporting freckles from a life spent outdoors. Not his type. He might have been born in Rocky Ridge, part of the Kiamichi mountain range, but he was a city boy through and through. The women he dated—when he had time, which wasn't too often—were educated, sophisticated, glamorous and preferably uninterested in marriage.

He checked his watch. Right on time. Where was his ride? he wondered irritably. He hated waiting. With a frustrated sigh he picked up his two bags and carried them across the runway to the dumpy building, which at least afforded a sliver of shade out of the bright, afternoon sun.

This didn't look like the Oklahoma he'd pictured, he thought as he looked around, the one with cattle and oil wells and gently rolling grassland. These were real moun-

ins, covered with green, verdant woods, with nary a cow
r drilling rig in sight. Nothing jarred his memory, but he'd
een only three when his parents had decided to relocate to
t. Louis.

As he paced a cracked slab of concrete near the empty
uilding, he tried to picture this ranch he'd inherited. The
robate lawyer had provided few details, other than the
ost important one—the operation was very nearly insol-
ent.

He heard the chug of an approaching vehicle with a mo-
or that needed a tune-up. He hoped it was his ride. An om-
ous bank of gray clouds gathered in the distance,
reatening to roll in across the mountains and ruin the
eautiful spring day. He wondered if he should dig out his
aincoat and umbrella. A drenching wouldn't do his wool
uit any good.

When he turned his attention back to the road, the ap-
roaching vehicle—a huge, incredibly old truck, so cov-
red with dust he couldn't discern its color—had just
ounded a bend. It heaved to a stop in front of him, and the
river, a slender woman, hopped out.

She was like a breath of fresh country air, as slender and
elicate as a blade of grass. Glossy brown hair, water
traight, hung loose to her shoulders and framed the per-
ect oval of her face. Her blue eyes were cool and serene, but
shock of unruly bangs suggested there was some mischief
bout her. Her mouth was wide and sensual, although at the
oment she wasn't smiling.

Her slim black jeans and teal blue cotton shirt were a far
ry from the overalls he'd expected. And she didn't have a
ingle freckle—not any he could see, anyway.

"Hello," she called to him in that distinctively lazy drawl.
"Welcome to Rocky Ridge." The voice had tickled his nerve
ndings even over hundreds of miles of telephone wire.

Combined with the face and body, it knocked his hor
mones into overdrive.

She approached him with an unconsciously hip-swinging
sexy gait, her hand extended. "I'm Ellie Kessler."

Her callused palm slid against his before their two hand
gripped each other more firmly for a quick shake. Hers wer
obviously hands accustomed to a hard day's work, yet tha
didn't detract from her femininity.

Quickly he found his voice. "I'm Zach Shaner, as I'r
sure you've figured out," he said, smiling.

She smiled back, but the expression seemed forced. Sh
was, perhaps, nervous at meeting her new "boss"? No, nc
nervous. She didn't seem the type. Her stride was too sur
as she stepped toward his luggage, her gestures fluidl
graceful. She picked up his duffel before he could protes
that he could handle all of it himself. With a shrug h
grabbed the heavier suitcase and followed her around th
truck.

The back of the vehicle was filled with big red-and-yello
sacks of something called Ratite Pellets.

Hmm. That sounded like feed of some sort. Or beddin
Or maybe it was fertilizer, what did he know? He should ju
ask Ellie exactly what sort of establishment the Red Car
yon Ranch was, but he was too embarrassed. She was h
employee. She would have no respect for him if he admi
ted that he hadn't even bothered to ask the probate atto
ney what sort of livestock he now owned.

He started to object when Ellie threw his brand-new Lou
Vuitton luggage in with the sacks, but he stopped himself i
time. Where else would the luggage go? There wasn't roor
in the cab.

"I don't suppose you could have collected me in som
thing smaller?" he joked as they climbed into the truck. H
wondered if he should have opened her door, then nixed th
idea. She seemed pretty capable.

"Nope. This is all that's available." As she said this, she gave him a quick, head-to-toe appraisal. "Are you worried about your suit? The truck's old, but I keep it clean—on the inside, at least."

"Yes, you do," he agreed. He was getting off on the wrong foot with the woman. Maybe he'd misread her tight smile earlier. He got the idea she wasn't nervous, but disapproving. He was making a bad impression, and he really wanted to get along with the ranch people.

No problem. As a financial troubleshooter, he was often thrust into the midst of a group of people who desperately needed his help and resented him all the same. He almost always won them over. In this case, however, when he announced he intended to dismantle the ranch, he wouldn't be the most popular guy around.

That couldn't be helped. The attorney had made it clear that the ranch, as a working concern, was losing money every day, and Zach didn't have the financial resources to carry it for long. Even if he had control of his trust fund, which he didn't, he wouldn't want to throw his legacy from his father into a bottomless pit.

He could try to sell the ranch intact, but it wasn't an attractive investment, and finding a buyer might take months. The land, on the other hand, was quite valuable to a theme-park developer who had expressed an interest in it. If he could get the right price, he could wipe out the ranch's debts, pay each employee a handsome severance stipend and have a little left over.

He returned his attention to his pretty little chauffeur, who did an admirable job wrestling with the gearshift of the unwieldy truck and maneuvering it along the narrow, twisting mountain roads. Ellie. The name suited her—casual and countrified, but feminine, too.

"So, Ellie, what position do you hold at the ranch?"

The question seemed to amuse her. "Position? I don't know. Clem never gave me an official title. Chief cook and bottle washer, I suppose."

"What exactly do you do?" Even if she did display a worn pair of cowboy boots on her feet, he couldn't quite picture her busting broncos or roping cattle—or whatever the hell people did on ranches.

She shrugged. "Whatever needs doing."

She was being deliberately vague, he decided. Well, he would see soon enough what function she served.

Ellie gave her passenger a sidelong glance. He was handsome, she had to admit, with a square jaw that jutted forward, hinting at a strong will, and a patrician nose that spoke of breeding she knew he didn't have. His kin were from Rocky Ridge, same as hers. His hair, thick and dark blond, was cut Madison Avenue short. Would long days spent in the sun sprinkle it with gold? she wondered. She probably would never know.

His eyes were green and hard to read. He would keep his cards close to his vest, she imagined.

Her appraisal moved lower, to his well-tailored and obviously pricey suit. He filled it out nicely, but his choice of clothing disappointed her all the same. She had been hoping Zach Shaner would turn out to be a beefy outdoorsman, one who could roll up his sleeves, pitch in, and help her turn the Red Canyon around. That possibility didn't appear likely. She hoped to heaven he'd packed some more useful clothing in one of those designer suitcases he'd brought.

"How far is it to the ranch?" Zach asked.

"'Bout an hour."

"An hour? This trip must have taken quite a chunk out of your day."

"Uh-huh."

He sighed. "I should have flown into Muskogee and ented a car."

"Then you might never have found the place," Ellie said. 'The Red Canyon is thirty minutes away from the nearest own."

He didn't appear thrilled over that news.

They traveled awhile in silence. Ellie concentrated on keeping the truck on the narrow, winding mountain roads. Zach gazed out the windows, taking it all in, she supposed. It would be impressive to a newcomer. Sometimes it still impressed her.

"This is beautiful country," he finally remarked, sounding surprised.

"What'd you expect?"

He shrugged. "My parents hardly ever talked about the place where they grew up, but when they did, they always gave me the impression that there wasn't much here of interest. They said it was backward. They talked about poverty and the lack of education and opportunity. They never mentioned how beautiful and unspoiled it was."

Ellie gritted her teeth. That attitude was all too typical of the ones who left and never came back. Yeah, this area had its problems, but rather than face those problems and try to correct them, most folks either escaped or stayed and accepted the status quo. Zach's parents represented the first group. Her own parents were from the second.

And she, Ellie Kessler, was a third group unto herself. She was trying to change things without undermining the very qualities that made Rocky Ridge unique.

"It won't stay unspoiled if some people get their way," she said, then wished she'd kept silent. She had decided that the best course of action was to show Zach all the good features of this wild countryside and its people, and then quietly state her case and hope for the best. If she started

arguing too soon, she might get his back up. After all, when
you push a man, he usually pushes back.

He gave her an oblique look but didn't rise to her bait.
Good. He apparently wasn't ready to argue. Maybe, just
maybe, that meant he hadn't yet made up his mind about
what to do with his new inheritance.

"We're almost there," Ellie said. "Over on the right is
Judd Whitsitt's place. He raises hogs. Wins a prize almost
every year at the state fair. And on the left is Roy and Mamie Rawlins's farm. They raise chickens. Do real well at it
too. My folks have chickens, but not half so many."

Hogs? Chickens? Zach tried not to let any trace of horror show on his face. Dear God, had he inherited a pig
farm? That vulgar possibility had never occurred to him.
"Doesn't anyone around here raise horses or cows?" he
asked, trying to sound casual. "I thought Oklahoma produced a lot of cattle."

She smiled wryly. "Farther west they do, but not as much
in these parts."

Zach got a sinking feeling in his stomach.

They were in a deep, tight valley, surrounded by steep
mountain walls that bore traces of the famed Oklahoma red
dirt. The ranch had been aptly named, Zach mused, but he
couldn't imagine how acreage of any appreciable size could
be squeezed into these confines.

He didn't fully realize his apprehension until Ellie made
a sharp turn, and he found himself looking up at a hand-painted sign that arched over the driveway, proclaiming this
the entrance to Red Canyon Ranch. On either side of the
driveway were small, empty pastures. At the end of it was
the strangest little house he'd ever seen. Or rather, two
houses, connected by a covered walkway of some sort. They
were both pretty pitiful looking.

Ellie put the truck in neutral. "Might as well pick up the
mail while I'm here," she said as she opened the door.

Overwhelmed with curiosity, Zach climbed out, too. He slammed the door closed behind him and walked around the front of the truck. Standing before the six-foot pipe-and-cable fence, he scanned the acreage beyond. From this vantage point, he could see that the property was larger than it had at first appeared, but it was long and narrow, following a flat ledge. Beyond the house he could see another drop-off, and he heard water running.

"What do you think?" Ellie called out to him.

"I'll reserve judgment." First he had to figure out whether he owned cows, chickens, hogs or elephants.

He took a deep breath, sniffing the air suspiciously. Surely if there were pigs nearby, he would smell them. But he smelled nothing except sweet, country air.

There, way in the distance, beyond a line of trees and brush, he saw something move. A bunch of somethings, big somethings, and they were black and white.

Cattle! it had to be. Optimism flowered inside his chest. So it wasn't a big, fancy ranch. At least he wasn't a pig farmer.

Ellie joined him at the fence. "What are you looking at?"

He pointed toward the animals. "Those. How many head are in there?" He was proud of himself for remembering the correct lingo.

"Head?" A faint smile touched her face. "Eighteen, last I counted."

Eighteen? Was that enough to be classified as a herd? Did this place even qualify as a ranch?

"'Course, then there are the emu. Got a dozen of the little guys in the west pasture."

"Oh, yes, of course." *E-moo?* No, emu, he corrected himself. He'd heard the word but couldn't remember what it meant. Maybe it was a miniature breed of cattle. Or something. He struggled to formulate an intelligent question. "And how many acres total? I've forgotten."

"A hundred and twenty. Most of those are vertical though," she added wryly. "Then there's that one hundred twenty-first acre, which may or may not belong to you. It depends on whose survey you believe. Your uncle Clem and his neighbor Ben Poteet have been squabbling over that one acre since before either of us was born."

"One acre? How ridiculous! Why don't they just turn it into a two-family cemetery and be done with it?" he quipped, then realized how tasteless his remark was in light of Clem's recent demise. "Er, I'm sorry. I didn't mean to—"

To his surprise, Ellie Kessler burst into laughter. "You know, you have more of Clem in you than I first thought. That's just like something he would have said."

Zach wasn't sure whether he'd been complimented or insulted, so he made no reply.

Ellie smiled again, a genuine smile this time. "Come on, let's get you settled in. Then I'll take you on the grand tour." She glanced down pointedly at his feet. "You *do* have some sensible shoes, I hope."

"Yes, and jeans, too," he said as they walked back to the truck. He realized now how inappropriately he was attired, but he'd been on a tight schedule which hadn't allowed him time to change into comfortable clothes. Ellie probably thought he was strange, showing up here in a suit.

Then again, he needed to impress upon her—and all the employees—that he was a businessman, and his decisions about the ranch were based on financial considerations, nothing more. Nothing personal.

Zach's introduction to the house, which Ellie explained was a "dogtrot," was an eye opener. The left half, which they entered first, included a formal living room and two bedrooms. Given the disreputable condition of the house's exterior, he had feared what the inside would reveal. But although it was in a 1930s time warp, complete with exposed wiring and Depression-era wallpaper and furniture, it appeared livable. It was clean, anyway.

He followed Ellie through the living room and into one of the small bedrooms. It was so full of furniture that there was little room to walk, and he found they were standing close enough that he caught her clean, feminine scent. He swallowed hard and took a step back until he was almost standing in the hallway.

"I made up the bed for you and kind of cleaned things up," Ellie said, leaning down to pick a minuscule piece of lint from the rag rug. "This was Clem's room—I hope you don't mind. But the other bedroom isn't near as comfortable."

Zach took stock of the cherrywood four-poster bed and matching armoire and dresser. They were heirloom-quality pieces, obviously lovingly cared for over many generations. Although he preferred the clean lines of his own contemporary furniture, he had to appreciate the fine grains revealed in the ornately carved surfaces.

"This is quite acceptable," he said. Then he frowned and asked, "My uncle didn't... expire in here, did he?"

Ellie grinned. "No, ol' Clem died as he lived, hard at work. One minute he was shoveling manure, the next he was gone, and that's exactly how he wanted it." Although Ellie's words were light, Zach sensed a sadness behind them.

"Were you close to him?"

Ellie shrugged one delicate shoulder. "Sure, I guess. Knew him all my life. He was a good friend of my folks, and I've been working here three years." She abruptly dropped the subject. "Listen, why don't you get changed and meet me in the other side of the house? That's where the kitchen is. We can decide what we want for dinner, and then I'll show you around."

He stepped back so she could exit. "Oh," he asked, "by the way, where's the bathroom?"

"There." She nodded toward a door at the end of the short hallway. "I'm afraid it's nothing fancy."

"I'm sure it's fine," he said as he headed toward the door.

Ellie turned, paused, almost said something, then stopped herself. She knew she should tell him. But a devilish part of her wanted to see his reaction to the primitive facilities.

She was rewarded with a horrified gasp. "Tell me you're kidding! Does this pump even work?"

Ellie came up behind him. "Of course it works. It pumps water up from the creek. Kinda cold, but it's crystal clean. Clem Shaner was quite a celebrity for a while back when he built this bathroom. First one around these parts with indoor plumbing."

Zach turned sharp green eyes on her. "Are you telling me there's not a..."

"Privy's out back." When he accepted this news with a stoic nod, guilt overcame her. "But there's a modern bathroom on the other side, attached to my quarters," she admitted. "You're welcome to use it whenever you want."

Any trace of acceptance vanished from his face, replaced by a fierce scowl. "Why didn't you tell me that in the first place? Freezing showers and... and *privies* are not my idea of fun."

"Oh, simmer down," she said good-naturedly. "I was just razzin' you a little."

He gave her a penetrating glare. "You don't like me, do you?"

"I barely know you, Zach," she said, mystified by the intensity of his reaction. She hadn't meant any real harm. "If the truth be known, I'm a little wary of you. You're an outsider, and I was raised to distrust outsiders. Not only that. You're holding my future, and that of a lot of other people, in your hands. But no, I don't dislike you. Not yet, anyway." With that parting shot she left.

FEATHERS AND LACE 19

Zach felt like a fool. Ellie had only been testing his sense of humor, and he had failed miserably. He wasn't normally such a bad sport. Perhaps he was more stressed out than he thought, what with the disruption of his schedule.

Yes, that was it. Latent stress. His doctor had told him he needed to reduce the pressure he put on himself and relax more, or he would have ulcers before he was thirty. Easy for the doctor to say. He didn't have deadline on top of deadline and a ranch he didn't want or need.

He quickly changed into a pair of crisp, seldom-worn jeans, a navy blue knit shirt, and loafers—his "sensible" shoes. He had a strange yen to be wearing cowboy boots. What self-respecting ranch owner wore loafers?

Maybe he would buy some boots while he was here, a souvenir of his brief stint as a cattle baron.

Smiling at the thought of what his friends would think, he went in search of Ellie to see what sort of damage control he could do there.

He found her in the kitchen, bent over an open deep freezer. She had changed, too, into a T-shirt and worn blue jeans—her work clothes, he supposed. Her hair was now pulled back into a ponytail, revealing the creamy column of her neck. As she leaned deeper into the freezer to forage, she gave him a splendid view of faded denim stretched invitingly across her... *Shaner, get a grip!* He wanted to convince her he was a purely professional businessman. Ogling his employees wouldn't enhance that image one bit.

"Chili all right for dinner?" she asked without looking up.

"Sure," he replied. He was determined to get on Ellie Kessler's good side. He would have said yes even if she'd suggested hog jowls and grits.

She brought out a package of meat and set it on the counter to thaw. Judging from the wrapping, it hadn't come from any supermarket. Zach wondered, but he didn't ask.

The kitchen was large, dominated by a big, square, pine table that was obviously homemade. Although scrupulously clean, the kitchen, too, appeared as if no one had updated it in sixty years. He wasn't surprised at the lack of a dishwasher or the ancient refrigerator, which looked to be one of the first electric models ever built. But a wood-burning stove?

"Do you actually cook on that?" he asked, pointing at the black monstrosity.

"Sure. It's not hard, once you get the hang of it. But for chili..." She reached into a lower cabinet and produced an electric slow-cooker. "You can't beat this."

While Ellie assembled her chili ingredients, Zach found the "modern" bathroom. Not luxurious by any stretch, it at least featured the necessary porcelain fixtures.

On his way back to the kitchen, he passed what was obviously Ellie's bedroom. The door was open, and he couldn't resist a long look inside as he walked slowly past. The furniture was basic oak. Everything was tidy, including the bed, which was covered with a Native American blanket. On the dresser sat a ceramic vase filled with large black-and-white feathers—an unusual accent, but maybe she wasn't the silk-flower type. Snapshots were tucked all around the dresser mirror.

Never one to be nosy, he moved along, although he wanted to know more. The woman was an enigma—a country girl with a drawl like warm honey, but wrapped in a sophisticated package. Her speech was liberally peppered with down-home expressions, but sometimes the grammar and vocabulary of an educated woman came out of her mouth. Born and raised here, perhaps, but educated elsewhere. If she got out once, why in heaven's name had she come back?

She was waiting for him by the front door.

"I'm ready," he said cheerfully, hoping to put his earlier, moody outburst behind them.

He was relieved when she smiled in return. She had a dimple on one side, he noticed. He had a silly, fleeting urge to touch it, to see how it would feel beneath his fingertip. Or to ruffle those unruly bangs, which were so charmingly out of sync with the rest of her neat appearance.

They took the big truck down a side road that led from the house along a fence line to a large, corrugated-tin building—a barn, he supposed. Several empty enclosures were attached to the barn. Corrals? Zach wondered as they got out of the truck. Horses! He had always liked horses, to look at, anyway. He'd never actually ridden one.

"I can unload the feed later," Ellie said. "Right now I imagine you're anxious to see the critters."

"Um, yes, actually." More anxious than she would ever know.

They went on foot the rest of the way, toward the line of trees he had noted earlier. He could still see the big black-and-white blobs moving through the foliage, along with some gray-brown ones. Every once in a while he saw a flash of pink.

Pink?

What in the world...?

As soon as they came around the line of trees, the pieces of the puzzle fell into place. There, milling around in the pasture, nibbling on grass and sipping from water troughs, were eighteen long-legged, long-necked, god-awful ugly creatures.

His mouth dropped open in an unsophisticated gape. "Oh, my God. Ostriches?"

Two

"Of course ostriches," Ellie replied, looking faintly amused. "What did you think?"

"Cattle. Horses. Even pigs. I just never suspected..." He was so dumbfounded he didn't even try to bluff his way through this. "Why ostriches?"

"Zach, you are looking at pure gold. The supreme growth market in livestock. The profit makers of the nineties."

The alleged profit makers were looking at him, too. Every one of those seven-foot birds had stopped what it was doing to stare curiously. Several were galumphing toward the fence, their small heads waving back and forth on pink, stalklike necks.

"But what do you do with them? Sell the feathers?"

"Eventually, when the industry matures. Someday Americans will be clamoring for the meat and leather, too. But right now it's a breeder's market. There's money to be made raising and selling the birds themselves to people who want to get into ostrich farming.''

One of the black-and-white birds came right up to the fence. After inspecting Zach up and down, it leaned over and snapped at his nose.

He jumped back. "Friendly, aren't they?"

"He's just curious. They're usually pretty mild mannered, unless they're breeding. Then the males get downright nasty. They can slice you open from stem to stern with one swipe of a foot. We're entering the breeding season now, so watch out."

Zach inspected this "mild-mannered" ostrich's feet. Each had two toes sporting wicked-looking nails. "I don't intend to get close enough that they can try any karate moves on me," he said. "Um, just exactly what is an emu?" He was willing to bet it wasn't a miniature cow.

"It's an Australian bird related to the ostrich, though quite a bit smaller. Same potential market. Want to see 'em?" She looked like a kid anxious to show off her new toys.

"Perhaps later," Zach replied as he tried to adjust his thinking. Ostriches. "How did my uncle Clem get into this? And if these birds are so great, how come the ranch is operating at a loss?"

Ellie's enthusiasm waned. "It's a long story." She gazed into the southwest, where the black clouds still threatened.

"I have all day."

"I need to get those sacks of feed unloaded and into the barn before the rain comes. If you want to hang around, I can tell you more about the ostriches while I work."

They walked back to the corrugated-tin building, where the truck was parked. Ellie opened the huge double doors and entered, with Zach right behind. He was more curious about this weird operation than he wanted to admit.

The barn didn't look like any he'd ever heard of. There were no horses, no stalls, no hayloft and no hay. Just a dim, cavernous interior housing various pieces of rusting farm equipment, an old horse trailer and what looked like fencing materials. The far end had been modified, housing several pens with access to the corrals he'd noticed earlier. Against another wall were a couple of huge, boxy, electrical contraptions of some sort.

"Those are the incubator and brooder," Ellie explained as she mounted a decrepit forklift and started it. "As soon as we get some eggs, we'll put 'em to good use." After waving Zach out of the way, she headed outdoors. He followed, his curiosity growing along with his fascination for the capable Ellie Kessler.

She climbed off the forklift and into the truck. With little fanfare, she grabbed one of the red-and-yellow bags by two corners and heaved it onto the lift. The ease and grace with which she worked indicated she had performed this ritual many times.

Good Lord, she was stronger than she looked, Zach thought. But strong or not, he refused to stand around and let her do the heavy work. He climbed up into the truck bed uninvited.

Ellie turned and stared at him, her eyebrows raised.

"I'll handle the bags," he said. "You do the forklift."

She nodded cautiously. "Okay."

He was awkward at first, but he soon got the hang of it. By the time she returned for the second load, he'd decided this physical labor felt good. He was challenging muscles that normally received only sporadic workouts at his health club.

"So, how did my uncle come to raise ostriches?" he asked.

"I guess you can blame me," Ellie said, glad to have something to distract her from the distinct pleasure of watching the poetry of Zach's body in motion. Lord knew she'd seen plenty of men engaged in physical work, but she'd never noticed how a man's muscles worked in concert with their neighbors to accomplish a task.

"Clem used to be a potato farmer," she continued, forcing herself to stare up at the darkening sky instead of at that lean, hard male. "He ran a few horses, too. Like everyone else around here, he scratched out a living from this miserable soil.

"Then a few years ago he came into a little bit of money from an insurance claim. He'd been in a car accident that messed up his back. Since it's hard to farm potatoes with a bum back, he was looking for a way to use that money to change his circumstances. I told him about ostriches, and he decided it was worth a try."

When the forklift was stacked high with another load of bags, Zach wiped his brow with the back of his hand, then peeled off his shirt, revealing an eyeful of smooth, golden skin stretched over those muscles.

Ellie realized she was staring. But how could she not? She averted her gaze even as she marveled at the undeniable effect his body had on her, a barely perceptible spiral of heat that tightened everything beneath her skin.

Abruptly she engaged the forklift in a three-point turn, then headed for a vacant corner of the barn. There she began stacking the sacks on top of a layer of wooden skids that kept them up off the ground.

"Why didn't Clem just make a new start somewhere?" Zach asked.

His voice startled her. She hadn't realized he'd followed her. But her surprise quickly gave way to irritation over his question. "Would you up and leave the land you'd worked for sixty years? The people you'd known all your life? For a man who'd never set foot outside Boone County, living somewhere else was unthinkable."

"I was only asking," Zach huffed. "After all, my parents were dissatisfied with their lot in life, so they left here with no prospects and not even any money, and they did all right for themselves."

"Just all right?" She had a feeling Zach was understating the case. He had a certain way about him, a certain ease and confidence that she'd noticed before among people who had grown up wealthy.

"More than all right. My father found his way into real estate. He was in the right place at the right time, and he built a comfortable life for his family."

"For some of his family." Ellie reminded herself to be patient. She couldn't expect him to instantly understand things it had taken her a lifetime to know.

"You sound disapproving."

"Do I? I suppose I can't help it. I have a hard time understanding why people abandon their roots."

"It's pretty easy to understand, the way I see it. When there's nothing but poverty and no opportunity, you *have* to leave. My dad said he tried for a number of years to make a living from a few scraggly apple trees. He had to supplement his income with seasonal work, following pipeline construction or timber harvesting, staying away from home for weeks at a time. And still he couldn't keep food on the table. I don't see anything wrong with abandoning *those* roots. My folks wanted something better for me, and frankly I'm damned glad they left."

Ellie sighed. "When you put it like that, I can understand their position," she admitted. "But you never even came back to visit. No one ever heard from your family again—including Clem, your father's own brother."

Zach's eyes again blazed with an angry green fire. "You make us sound like a bunch of creeps. Maybe the brothers had a falling out. I never even knew there *was* a Clem Shaner until two weeks ago. Maybe they were too embarrassed to come back after they made a little money. Hell, at this point, who knows? But my parents were good people, regardless of what you've heard. And I won't stand by and let you—"

"Were?" Oh, dear. What had she done?

"Yeah, they're both dead. They would have to be, for me to inherit this place."

"Oh." Now it was Ellie who felt like a creep. "I'm sorry, Zach. I had no business talking about your kin that way. I never even knew them. I was just carrying tales. It's a bad habit."

He nodded, appreciating the fact that she could admit when she was wrong. So many people couldn't. "Let's unload the rest of the feed. Sounds like the wind's picking up."

It occurred to Zach, as they dealt with the last of the feed bags, that Ellie might be partly right about his parents. They'd been proud, often arrogant, people. He could see them ruthlessly turning their backs on an unkind past.

It also occurred to Zach that, if his father and uncle had had a falling out, Clem Shaner would never have intended for his nephew to inherit anything of his. He probably would have preferred to have left everything to Ellie, with whom he'd apparently shared a great deal. Too bad the old man hadn't made out a will. If there were any way for Zach to simply sign the whole thing over to Ellie, he'd do it in a heartbeat. Then again, the operation was about to come crashing down. Ownership wouldn't improve her lot.

The first fat raindrops began to fall as Ellie shut off the forklift. "We better make a run for it," she told Zach as she climbed down. "Unless you want to be stranded here while the storm blows through."

"No, thanks." He pulled his shirt over his head.

After silently appraising the rate of rainfall, Zach walked briskly to the truck and opened Ellie's door for her—just to show her there were no hard feelings over their argument.

As soon as they'd both climbed inside and slammed the doors, the skies opened up.

There was something intimate about sharing the cab of a truck with a woman while rain pelted the roof and thunder rumbled in the distance, Zach mused. He could smell the faint, flowery scent emanating from her damp hair. An errant raindrop had landed on her nose, and he felt an insane urge to kiss it off.

Son of a gun. He was attracted to the woman. She would probably sock him right in the jaw if she knew what he was thinking.

"Will the ostriches be okay?" he asked, a frown line forming between his eyebrows.

Ellie started the truck. "There's a shelter in the pasture. But some of the stupid things won't even get under it. They don't seem to mind the rain, and the emu absolutely love a good downpour. They're all hardy animals. They can subsist on the most barren rangeland, and extreme temperatures don't bother them a bit."

"Then they ought to get along fine here," Zach commented. "I've heard Oklahoma can get hot in the summer and cold in the winter."

"That's exactly why I wanted to introduce them to this area." She backed the truck around and headed slowly toward the house, peering through a layer of rain that the old wipers couldn't begin to keep pace with. "Ostriches can thrive where little else will, and they don't need a lot of room. You can keep a dozen birds on an acre of land. The food is cheap—one adult bird eats less than a dollar's worth per day. And generally they're easy to care for. I've been doing all the work myself since Clem died, and it hasn't been too bad."

"You mean you're the ranch's only employee?" At first Zach had visualized a bunkhouse full of cowboys. As reality had slowly seeped in, he had thought maybe the ranch had day workers.

"I'm it."

"Are other farmers around here raising ostriches?" he asked.

"Not yet. They're all watching the Red Canyon to see what happens. So far no one is overly impressed. But they will be, soon as the hens start laying eggs. That could be anytime."

"And then what happens?"

At least he sounded genuinely curious, Ellie thought. And he seemed a lot more touchable now that he wore something besides that stiff businessman suit. She was surprised that he'd pitched in to help with the feed bags. Maybe there was hope for him yet.

She parked the truck in front of her half of the house. "We sell the eggs and start paying off a few debts."

"Eggs, huh?" She could tell he was pondering just how much income a few eggs could bring. "What do you do with ostrich eggs, make giant omelets?"

"You could, I suppose," Ellie said with mock seriousness. "They say one egg can make omelets for eight people. But it would be a mighty expensive meal, seeing as one egg is worth about a thousand dollars."

Zach's jaw dropped. "You're kidding."

"A pair of chicks, on the other hand, can go for about six thousand. And a mature breeding pair—" she paused before dropping her pièce de résistance "—can sell for seventy thousand dollars."

"Do you mean to tell me that herd of feathers out there . . ."

"Is worth four hundred thousand dollars, give or take a dime or two. Add in the emu, and you have easily a half million dollars in livestock."

"Could you actually sell them for that?" Zach asked.

Ellie didn't like the sound of that question. He might be asking out of curiosity—or he might be calculating how many BMWs and trips to Europe he could get out of this windfall.

She answered carefully. "If given the time, yeah, I could sell them for top dollar once they're actually breeding. But that would be a damn shame. Clem and I bought most of those birds when they were just a few weeks old. We poured every resource we had between us into raising them to this stage. Now that they're ready to start paying dividends, they can produce income for decades to come. They live forty or fifty years, you know."

"No, I didn't know." He made a swift exit from the truck and dashed inside.

Ellie chuckled. She'd given him plenty to chew on. She would wait before launching the next salvo.

"This chili is great," Zach said. They were seated at the big kitchen table with bowls of the fragrant stuff topped with grated cheddar cheese. Also on their plates were thick slices of freshly baked corn bread and cooked turnip greens, all of which Ellie had whipped up in almost no time. "And this corn bread—I've never tasted anything like it."

"You've never had corn bread?" Ellie asked, in a tone of voice that indicated she rated skillet corn bread right up there with mom and apple pie.

"I've had it, but it was always more like cake—sweet and fluffy. This is hard and chewy and..." He stopped to take another butter-slathered bite.

"And it'll stick to your ribs," Ellie finished for him. "That's what my ma says. She's the one who taught me to fix it that way."

"And the chili?"

"Same thing. The worst part about Clem dying, according to my mother, is that now I don't have anyone to cook for. Her views on a woman's role in society are a little backward."

"Mmm, you can cook for me anytime," Zach said. This food might not be what he was used to in St. Louis, but it was satisfying.

"You're not eating your greens," Ellie pointed out.

"No, I guess I'm not." He politely refrained from explaining that the turnip greens tasted like boiled grass clippings. Some country cooking he liked, but not that slimy stuff.

Ellie didn't pursue it. "So, what else do you need to know about the Red Canyon?" she asked.

"Well, I suppose I should take a look at the books and see how bad things really are." At her uneasy expression he added, "You do keep books, right?"

"Yeah . . ."

"Then what's the problem?"

"No problem, really. It's just that I haven't had a chance to explain to you in depth about the finances. You see, Clem didn't plan very well for his death. It's not something either of us thought about. When he died, all of his assets were frozen. At that point I had no choice but to start doing some rather creative maneuvering. The birds had to eat and so did I."

"What sort of maneuvering?" Zach asked, senses alert. He didn't think Ellie was the type to be monkeying with the books, but what did he really know about her, after all?

"Bartering. Horse trading. I get a freezerful of meat, feed pellets and gas for the truck. My neighbors get a future interest in the first eggs produced at the Red Canyon. Each unlaid egg has five hundred shares at a dollar apiece. If I sell it for a thousand dollars, the investors have doubled their money. It's a little unorthodox, but perfectly legal. It just looks weird on the profit-and-loss statement."

"You mean you've been running things without any cash? What about the electric bill? Taxes? And what about your salary?"

"Taxes aren't due yet. The electric bill is, well, overdue. And I haven't received a salary in over a year," she admitted.

"And you still work here?" It seemed a perfectly logical question to him, yet Ellie looked at him like he needed a brain transplant.

"Of course I still work here. This is my life! This is what I want to do. Can you understand what it means to do something just because you love it? Because it's important? The money doesn't matter. The continuing success of the ranch does."

He dabbed at his mouth with a napkin. "Don't get so bent out of shape. As a matter of fact, I do understand what it means to do something for love."

"Like what?" she prodded.

He hadn't thought about his former avocation in a long time. An achy nostalgia washed over him. "I used to build furniture," he said softly. "I was damned good at it, too, but it wasn't exactly a profit-making venture. My parents despaired of my ever making a success of myself. In college I did more sanding than studying."

"Why couldn't you be a success as a furniture builder?"

"I might have made a living, eventually, but I was impatient. Anyway, carpentry wasn't what my father considered a 'useful' occupation. So, dutiful son that I was, I managed to get a degree in finance, and found a better way to earn my bread and butter."

"And you quit making furniture?" Ellie appeared disturbed over that prospect.

"I still work on a piece now and then." Although, come to think of it, he hadn't turned on his lathe in probably three years. He just didn't seem to have the time anymore.

Ellie took a second helping of greens. "Then maybe you do understand." She met his gaze with soft blue eyes, eyes that reflected naked hope.

He had to look away. He wasn't quite sure what she was asking for, but he had a gnawing suspicion that it wasn't his to give. "Sometimes passion has to give way to practicality," he said, knowing it wasn't what she wanted to hear.

She cleared her throat, signaling a return to more immediate concerns. "When you look at the books, you'll also see that I've put quite a bit of my own money into the operation. But I want you to know I have no intention of making any claim to the profit, once the ranch starts making one."

He looked at her curiously. She was awfully intense about this. What was the big deal if she'd put a few dollars into feed pellets? "I believe you."

She settled back in her chair. "I won't lie to you. Things are in pretty bad shape. Clem and I had it figured down to the penny how much money we would need before we started seeing a return—and it would have worked out just fine if he hadn't up and died. Death is expensive."

"Yes, I know." He remembered all too vividly the thousands upon thousands of dollars that had gone into straightening out his father's estate, and then his mother's a few years later.

"I have some cash," he said, thinking aloud. "I can probably keep the wolves at bay for a little while, but...well, it seems obvious, doesn't it? I'll have to sell this place as soon as possible."

Ellie's mouth tightened into a thin, white-rimmed line. "I see."

"I want to do right by you, too. I can assure you, if you've invested in this ranch, you'll get some kind of return."

"I just told you, I'm not in this for the money!" She pounded her fist on the table, hard enough to rattle the dishes. "Dammit, I should have known you would go for the fast buck."

He sat up straighter. "I beg your pardon?"

She quickly backpedaled. "I just meant that I shouldn't have expected a city person, an outsider, to have the same interest in keeping this place running that I do. It's nothing against you personally."

Then why did he have the feeling that her comment had been distinctly personal? He wasn't stupid. He knew when he'd been insulted. "Ms. Kessler," he said in his most controlled voice, "I want you to know that I view this inheritance as a nuisance, not as a windfall. I have a life back in St. Louis, a career. It's obvious that you would like to keep the ranch going. That's understandable. You've put a lot of work into it. But be reasonable. I'm no ostrich farmer. You can't expect me to pour my own money into something I have no interest in. I have no choice but to sell."

"To SunnyLand, Inc., perhaps?"

So, Ellie knew all about the developer who was interested in building the SunnyLand Choctaw Park on this land. "I intend to talk to them, yes. It's only prudent that I explore all my options. But I haven't made a final decision yet. When I do, I promise you I will take *all* circumstances into account, including yours."

Ellie hardly looked mollified. She tapped her spoon restlessly against the edge of her bowl, staring into space.

Zach wished they could reclaim their earlier mood. This deadly silence put him on edge.

With a sigh he poured another ladleful of chili into his bowl. His appetite certainly hadn't suffered since he'd arrived here. Maybe it was the country air.

"I can't get over how good your chili is," he said, knowing it was a lame attempt at shifting the conversation to safer topics. "What's your secret?"

To his surprise, a slow smile spread across Ellie's face. "It's a blend of spices handed down in my family for generations. But I think the real difference is the squirrel meat."

Zach's spoon clattered to the table as he fought the urge to gag.

Three

─────

Ellie honked the horn of the old truck impatiently. It was bad enough that Zach was headed into Ledbetter to meet with SunnyLand's Phyllis Quincy, a woman who wanted to make a fast tourist buck by scarring Rocky Ridge with a stupid amusement park. It was worse that she, Ellie Kessler, was driving him into town so he could keep the appointment.

But Zach would never have found his way through the twisted maze of unnamed roads by himself, at least not the first time. Besides, she had to run a few of her own errands in town. And she was still feeling guilty over the squirrel meat.

She hadn't meant to make him sick. She'd just wanted to rattle his cage a bit when she'd told him what was in the chili. But she'd forgotten how truly vile most city people thought squirrel meat was. She had never seen anyone's face turn quite that shade of green.

Ellie had felt a momentary sense of triumph, followed by a tidal wave of guilt. Her ma had raised her to be a lady, and a lady did not deliberately turn a dinner guest's stomach.

When Zach had recovered, she'd apologized profusely for not warning him about the small amount of squirrel meat that had gone into the chili. He had accepted her apology with a tight-lipped nod.

Shortly after, he had taken a brief look at the Red Canyon's books, frowning the whole time. He hadn't said much, and that worried her. She wasn't quite sure what Zach did for a living, but it had something to do with finance. It obviously hadn't taken him long to figure out just how far in debt the ostrich operation was.

First thing this morning he had announced his intention to meet with Ms. Quincy. Ellie still wasn't sure whether he had made the appointment ahead of time or whether the sight of all that red ink had prompted him to call the developer's representative and speed things along.

She honked again.

"I'm coming, I'm coming," he said irritably as he hurried outside. He paused to look at the front door, shrugged, then joined her in the truck. He was once again the stern-looking, no-nonsense Mr. Businessman in his dove gray suit, starched white shirt and maroon silk tie. He was wearing after-shave, too, a citrusy, not-too-sweet scent that spoke to the woman in her. It wrapped around her senses, teasing her like a feather.

Would it tease Phyllis Quincy's senses? she wondered, feeling an irrational but definite tug of jealousy. She shouldn't be jealous, though. There wasn't a single chance Zach would reach Ms. Quincy's heart. The woman didn't have one.

"Your front door doesn't have a lock," Zach observed as he settled himself on the cracked leather seat, positioning an eelskin briefcase across his lap.

"No need for one. Folks around Rocky Ridge may b
poor, but they're mostly honest."

"It seems odd, just driving away and leaving everythin
open."

"I'd think it would be even more odd, having to fear fo
your valuables every time you turn your back. How man
dead bolts do you have on your door at home?"

He pressed his lips together in a frown. "Two. But wha
if someone stole the birds?" he persisted.

Ellie grinned at the thought of bird rustlers. Oh, it cer
tainly wasn't unheard of, particularly in areas where raisin
exotic birds was a common enterprise. But around here..

"Someone could try, I suppose, but I'd lay odds no on
from Rocky Ridge would have the first idea how to herd on
of those ornery beasts into a trailer."

He smiled at the verbal picture she painted.

"Besides, it's not easy to unload a hot ostrich. You can'
exactly sell one on a street corner."

"Or hock it at a pawn shop," he agreed. "Listen, Ellie,
appreciate your taking the time to drive me into town," h
said, returning to his business-polite voice. "Knowing hov
you feel about Ms. Quincy—"

"You have no idea the depths of my feelings for Ms
Quincy," Ellie said, interrupting, her hands tightenin
around the steering wheel.

"Really? Tell me about her."

Ellie had promised herself she wasn't going to do this. I
she got started talking about the proposed theme-park de
velopment, she was liable to become completely irrational
It made her crazy to think about outsiders taking advan
tage of this unspoiled wilderness just to line their owr
pockets. But since he'd asked...

She put the truck in gear and stamped down on the ac
celerator. "Phyllis Quincy is a vulture who'll do anything
for a buck. For two years she tried to get Clem to sell the

Red Canyon. Clem wouldn't consider it, of course, so the clever Ms. Quincy moved to Plan B.''

"Plan B?" Zach's eyebrows drew together.

"She started out with a little friendly harassment—endlessly pointing out how ridiculous the ostrich-ranch idea was, how Clem stood to lose every dime. Persuasive arguments, outlandish promises, enticements of everything from new cars to European vacations. I think she even offered sex. But Clem wasn't interested.

"So she got out the big guns. There were physical threats—graffiti painted on the barn, anonymous phone calls. A grass fire started mysteriously in an empty pasture, and someone shot one of the emu.''

"Shot? As in killed?" Zach's eyes darkened to forest green. "But surely that wasn't Ms. Quincy's doing. She seems like a very nice, very professional woman. Maybe it was just a random act of vandalism.''

Ellie shrugged. "I can't prove anything." But she knew. "Just watch your step. And don't sign anything until a lawyer goes over it with a magnifying glass.''

"Ms. Kessler, I can assure you I'm not an idiot when it comes to legal matters. Contracts are very much a part of my business.''

So, he was back to calling her Ms. Kessler. She wished he would loosen up. If he had even a little of Clem in him, he could open his eyes to the possibilities...ah, hell, what was the use? Apparently when they took the boy out of the country, they took the country out of the boy, as well.

"Just a little friendly warning, that's all," she said. "I can't stop you from selling the Red Canyon, if that's what you're aiming to do. But...don't rush, okay?''

"As I told you last night, I intend to explore all the options," he said. "Speaking of which, if you really don't want me to sell, you might be thinking of some alternatives. I'm not immune to the powers of persuasion. And something tells me you can be pretty persuasive when you want to be." He accompanied this provocative observation with a half smile and a flicker of interest in those mysterious eyes.

Was Mr. No-nonsense Businessman flirting with her?

Nah, that was ridiculous. Intriguing thought, but not possible. Even so, her blood pulsed a little harder at the thought that he might be interested in her as a woman.... Nah.

He had a point. So far she'd been long on rhetoric, spouting lots of philosophical reasons he should want to preserve what his forebears had built, but she'd been short on concrete alternatives.

Maybe that was because there weren't any, an inner voice pointed out.

She shushed the voice. Hell, she'd been operating on nothing but grit and optimism and a silver tongue for months now. There was no reason to believe she couldn't keep it up. Any day now. Any day those infernally slow beasts would start laying eggs. If she could show Zach just one egg, one tangible piece of evidence that her plan wasn't a pipe dream, she *knew* she could convince him not to sell.

She pulled the truck in front of Rosie's Café, where Zach had arranged to meet Phyllis Quincy.

"You don't have to wait for me," he said, opening the door. "I know you have work to do. I can get a ride back. Maybe Ms. Quincy can take me."

Ellie winced inwardly at the thought. She didn't want those two getting any more chummy than was necessary.

"Or I could take a cab," he suggested when she remained silent.

She laughed at that. "Zach, honey, there's not a cab within a hundred miles of here. Don't worry, I have things to keep me busy. I'll be at the Laundromat." And while she did her laundry, she would do some thinking on what sort of proposition she could make Zach that would rival the oily Ms. Quincy's deep pockets. Some powerful thinking.

Zach exited Rosie's Café an hour later, his briefcase heavier and his heart lighter. This was going to work out beautifully. He could hardly wait to tell Ellie everything he'd found out by talking with Phyllis Quincy.

He couldn't understand why his uncle had been so adamant about not dealing with the woman. True, Phyllis did exude a certain slickness. She was out to make a buck, no doubt about it. But weren't most people?

As he walked down the cracked sidewalk, he took notice of downtown Ledbetter for the first time. It wasn't a bad little town, he decided. It was neat and clean, and with its many shops, selling everything from candy to local Indian crafts, it had a certain touristy appeal to it. When summer arrived, bringing hundreds of vacationers to nearby Lake Takanachi, the sidewalks would be crowded with families intent on spending money. If it weren't for the tourists, this town probably would have died a long time ago, he mused.

That's where the future lay for this depressed area—the tourist industry. SunnyLand, Inc. was going to help build that future—if it could gain cooperation from some of the more narrow-minded locals.

According to Phyllis, his uncle Clem hadn't even bothered to look at the plans. Neither had Ellie. Surely once Ellie understood what exactly the theme park entailed, and what it would mean to the local economy, she wouldn't be so dead set against it.

He found her inside the Laundromat, engaged in an animated conversation with an elderly woman as they worked together folding sheets. Zach stood in the doorway and silently watched as the two women exchanged easy banter. The afternoon sun shone through a window at Ellie's back, forming a rich halo around her head and casting the rest of her body into glorious silhouette.

At that moment, Zach realized that in addition to her heart-stopping looks, Ellie Kessler was an amazing woman. He'd been so busy sparring with her, defending himself against her more cutting remarks, that he hadn't taken time to appreciate the person she was. It was rare to find someone who wasn't interested in personal gain, someone who cared so deeply about her family and neighbors that she practically bankrupted herself to finance a crazy dream.

And it wasn't only her dream. She had planted seeds of interest all over the community. Enriching the area through ostrich and emu ranching had become a collective dream, if this old woman's attitude was any indication.

"Just think of the mountain of meringue I could make from one of them eggs," the woman said, shaking her head. "Let me buy some shares. Most all of my kin own eggs, now, an' I'm feelin' left out."

Ellie laughed. "Well, now, what have you got to trade?"

"I got cash money!"

"Bessie, I can't let you go speculating with your hard-earned cash."

"It wasn't hard-earned," she argued. "It's birthday money from my granddaughter, and she told me to spend it on whatever I please. It pleases me to own part of an ostrich egg." She dropped the folded sheet into her torn plastic laundry basket, then folded her arms across her ample chest, assuming a stubborn stance. "Ellie Kessler, everyone knows you're as cash poor as a church mouse on welfare. You need this money, and I'm aimin' to invest in an egg, and that's all there is to it."

Ellie shrugged, defeated. Zach suspected she had intended to give in all along. "All right, Bessie. How much money is it?"

"Ten dollars!" she announced proudly.

From the doorway, Zach cleared his throat, announcing his presence as Bessie dug into her coin purse.

"Oh, hello," Ellie said. "Zach, this is Bessie Peebles. She works at the candy store down on the corner. Bessie, this is Zach Shaner."

Zach extended his hand. "It's nice to—"

"This the one you were tellin' me about?" Bessie asked, absently handing a ten-dollar bill to Ellie as she stared intently at Zach with sharp black eyes. "Jerry and Frannie's boy?"

Ellie nodded.

Reluctantly Bessie shook Zach's hand. "Welcome to Ledbetter," she said, forcing the words out through tight lips.

"Thank you," Zach responded with similar reserve. He knew when he'd been snubbed. "Are you ready to go?" he asked Ellie, giving her a pointed look.

"Sure." As she picked up her own laundry basket, she turned toward Bessie. "I'll let you know when your egg gets laid."

As soon as they were inside the truck, Zach exploded. "What did you tell that woman about me? She looked at me like I was the devil himself!"

Ellie jumped to her own defense. "I didn't tell her anything, except that you were Clem's nephew and you inherited the Red Canyon."

"And that I was thinking of selling to SunnyLand," he added.

"I didn't tell her that. As a matter of fact, that's something I'd rather people didn't know about. I would lose all my bartering leverage."

It took a few moments for Zach to understand what she was saying. If he sold the ranch, those shares in future eggs she bartered with would be worthless. There would be no eggs. The ostriches would have to be sold.

"No one's going to lose their money," he said. "I'll personally guarantee any shares already on the books. And Bessie's, too."

She gave him a sideways look, as if trying to grasp the true meaning behind his words. "But I shouldn't trade away any more, is that what you mean? Are you selling out?"

"Can you give me a reasonable alternative?" he asked. He almost hoped she could. His optimism about Phyllis Quincy's offer had faded during the last few minutes.

"Can you live with your conscience?"

"My conscience won't bother me at all. No one is going to get a raw deal from me. After talking with Phyllis, I'm convinced the theme park is a good idea."

"So, it's 'Phyllis' now, is it?"

He did a double take. Ellie's voice bore the strangest note in it—not just anger or disgust, but something more like . . . jealousy? *Don't be ridiculous, Zach. Ellie Kessler can't stand you.*

"Could we go somewhere and discuss this reasonably?" he asked. "How about that pizza place I saw coming into town? I haven't had lunch." And he wouldn't make the mistake of trusting his stomach to Ellie's freezer again.

"Didn't you and Phyllis 'do lunch'?"

"We were too busy talking. Do you want pizza or not? It's my treat," he added.

"Well, now, I guess a poor country girl like me can't turn down a free lunch."

"I give up," he said, crossing his arms. "You're determined to see me in the worst possible light. You won't listen to anyone but yourself, even if they have solutions to problems you'd never thought of."

Her only reaction was a slight firming around her shapely mouth.

Her stubbornness, her refusal to bend, riled him like nothing else could. "Well, fine, then, to *hell* with you. I'll sell the land *and* the birds to SunnyLand. They've offered me a fair price for the whole lot of 'em. I'll pay off the ranch's debts, including your back salary, and we'll be rid of each other. Does that suit you?"

"You know damn well it doesn't!"

"Then let's talk about this! Lord, you're as stubborn as a mule on Sunday."

Whatever he'd said, it defused the anger. Ellie threw back her head and laughed. "Where did you get that?" she finally managed.

"Get what?" he asked, confused.

"'Stubborn as a mule on Sunday.'"

"I...I don't know. It just popped out." Not from his upbringing, certainly. His parents both had carefully cultivated all traces of a Southern accent out of their speech. And his mother, especially, had monitored his grammar, doggedly correcting every minor error. Zach hadn't been allowed to use slang. Even local colloquialisms were frowned upon. She had reminded him, time and again, that sloppy speech marked one as a hick, uneducated, even stupid.

"I'll make a deal with you, Zach," Ellie said. "I'll listen to whatever it is you have to say. And I'll try to have an open mind, although...no, I'll just have an open mind. But then you have to listen to my side—why Clem and I started the ranch, and what I hope to accomplish with it. And you have to keep an open mind, too. I have my own ideas about how you ought to deal with your inheritance."

Zach nodded. "Sounds fair." That's all he'd been asking for, a chance to be heard. Then why did he have this uneasy feeling that when Ellie was finished talking, his choices wouldn't be so easy?

By the time the waitress brought their large pepperoni pizza, they had reached a peaceful truce, agreeing to post-

pone their inevitable arguments about the ranch until after
they'd eaten.

"Where did you go to college?" Zach asked as he used a
fork to cut the point off his first piece.

"How do you know I went to college?" Ellie countered.
She watched him pop that minuscule bite into his mouth,
neat as you please, and chew, oh, so quietly. The man had
table manners, she'd give him that.

He wiped his mouth with a paper napkin. "It shows."

She nodded, conceding him the point. "I went to Western Oklahoma, to learn all about how to be a chicken
farmer. My folks had a few chickens, and I was convinced
that raising poultry was the wave of the future for Rocky
Ridge."

"It didn't turn out that way?"

"No. I found out you can't make much money from
chickens unless you're a large-scale producer. So I studied
zoology and looked around for something I could bring
home with me, something that would change Rocky Ridge
without *changing* it."

"Is this part of your pitch?" he asked suspiciously.

"Well, yeah, but you asked."

He motioned with his fork. "Go on. Why did you feel
you had to change things?"

"If you'd grown up here, you wouldn't have to ask. This
is one of the most beautiful places on earth. It's also one of
the poorest in the country. A lot of the kids get the hell out
as fast as they can, leaving their parents with no one to help
them work their farms and their—"

"Like my parents did," he said.

"People do what they have to do. I'm not condemning
them." Although perhaps she was. Zach had heard the
censure in her voice or he wouldn't have jumped in so defensively.

"Go on," he said, meeting her gaze with one of defiance.

Damn, she couldn't go on now. She had insulted his parents—for the second time—and thus had insulted him. That wasn't nice or fair of her. She hadn't known Jerry and Frannie, and most of the opinions she held about them were from the bits and pieces her own parents and Clem had let drop over the years. Based on that, she had judged and condemned Zach right along with his folks.

Zach was loyal to them; that was plain to see. He was true to his roots—the ones in St. Louis—and that was commendable. He just didn't know, yet, where all of his roots lay. Until yesterday, he'd hardly known of Rocky Ridge's existence.

"Does everyone around here hate me because my parents left?" Zach asked. The question was matter-of-fact, but Ellie sensed a certain discomfort in it. "That woman, Bessie. Is that why she was so cold to me?"

"It's more a case of you being an outsider...." Ellie began, but how could she explain such an ingrained attitude?

"They left here because they wanted something more for me than they'd been given. They wanted good schools and a nice house with a roof that didn't leak. They wanted choices and opportunities for themselves—they loved to go to the ballet and the opera. I don't see what's so wrong with that."

"There is *nothing* wrong with that," Ellie said to assure him, really meaning it this time. Most people want something better for their children than they had for themselves, but few had the guts to go after it. "I'm sorry. My feelings about this place run deep, and sometimes I get carried away." She reached across the table and laid her hand on his, hoping he would understand that it was a gesture of friendship.

She was surprised that he didn't resist her touch. In fact, he took her hand and squeezed it. And the way he looked at her, sort of yearninglike... She was glad they were in the middle of a pizza parlor. If they'd been anywhere more private, she firmly believed Zach might have leaned across the table and kissed her.

Fat chance, Ellie. How could she insult the man's parentage and then expect him to hold her in anything but contempt?

Abruptly Zach pulled his hand away. He cast about for something to do, eventually settling on adjusting his tie. He looked anywhere but at her.

"It doesn't matter," he finally said. "My parents always claimed they didn't fit in. I guess it's true. If the people here are so narrow-minded that they judge me for where I came from instead of who I am, that's their problem. I don't care."

But he did care. It showed in his eyes. And that meant that Rocky Ridge was getting to him. On some level he recognized his birthplace and wanted to belong.

It was a start. And it gave her hope—hope that he might come to see things her way, and that he could learn to love this land and these good, simple folk. Hope that he might want to redeem himself in the eyes of his people by helping turn their dreams into reality.

Four

―――

"And SunnyLand has pledged to invest some of their profits in the community," Zach said, waving his arms emphatically. "They'll earmark a certain percentage for civic improvements, better roads and conservation efforts. They'll even offer low-interest mortgage loans with easy qualifying to area residents, so they can afford their own homes."

"Most of the people in Rocky Ridge already own their own homes, such as they are," Ellie grumbled, toying with a piece of pizza crust. She'd been listening to Zach extol the virtues of the SunnyLand Choctaw Park for the past twenty minutes.

"They can get home-improvement loans, then," he continued, undeterred by her glumness.

She wondered if he realized that once the park became a reality, her home—the Red Canyon—would be bulldozed into so much rubble. Some improvement.

"Then there's education," he said. "SunnyLand will establish a scholarship fund—"

"That all sounds fine and good," Ellie said, unable to make herself listen to another word. "Ms. Swivel-hips Quincy obviously has a very convincing line of bull. But will SunnyLand actually keep those promises?"

"It's all in writing," Zach explained patiently, taking her grousing in stride. "The company is legally obligated to the government and its investors to follow through with these programs exactly as they've been outlined. Phyllis produced very adequate documentation."

"And did she also tell you about the lawsuits?"

Zach's handsome face, animated moments before with enthusiasm, went blank. "What lawsuits?"

"The ones in Arkansas, where they put in their first theme park. It seems the jobs they promised for the community never materialized. They brought in all their own people for management positions and left only the low-paying work for the locals. They're also being sued over a polluted creek, one that many residents depended on for their livelihood. All the fish died."

That silenced Zach.

Ellie took her opportunity. "Let's go. I want to take you on a little tour." She would drive them back to the ranch via the scenic route. Zach could see for himself the magnificent mountain vistas and rainbows of wildflowers threatened by development. More important, however, she intended to show him the *real* Rocky Ridge.

The first stop on the tour was a scenic lookout, not much more than a wide place in the dirt road. Ellie parked the truck and got out, feeling that peculiar exhilaration that only this land could give her. The air, growing warm on this April afternoon, was redolent with the scent of honeysuckle. All around them was a palette of wildflower col-

ors—dogtooth violets, wild iris, trillium—and dogwood
blossoms, scattered like white lace among the trees.

She led Zach to the edge of a cliff, where emerald forest-
land stretched out before them in an endless sea of rolling
green hills. Below them a creek tumbled over a precipice,
creating a waterfall that spread out like a white horse's tail.

To Ellie the view was as familiar as her own face in the
mirror. So instead she studied Zach. He had removed his
jacket and tie in deference to the day's warmth, rolling up
the pristine white sleeves to reveal his muscular forearms.
His skin was a natural golden color, not pale, but not tanned
by the sun, either. She suspected he didn't ordinarily spend
much time outdoors. His shirt was open at the collar, revealing a tantalizing tuft of springy golden chest hair.

At the moment, however, it was the expression on his face
that most interested her. Although he obviously was attempting to school his features, he couldn't hide what was
in those green eyes of his. He was awed by the view.

"If you're trying to convince me how picturesque this
place is," he said, "I've already figured that out."

"I just want to keep that thought fresh in your mind," she
returned. "Did you know we're standing on property now
owned by SunnyLand? Before long, we'll have to pay an
admission price to appreciate this view—if the view exists
anymore."

"They do a good job of blending their construction with
the scenery," Zach said with slightly less enthusiasm than
he'd shown before. "They take out as few trees as possible.
Phyllis showed me pictures of some of their other parks."

"I'll bet she didn't show you any pictures of parking lots.
But that's what they'll make of the Red Canyon. A damn
parking lot." She spat out the words with disgust.

Zach made no further comment.

Once they were on the road again, Ellie drove slowly
through a small pocket of civilization, waving to an occa-

sional neighbor who looked up from gardening to notice the truck's passage. She gave Zach plenty of time to appreciate the poverty—tar-paper shacks, log cabin dogtrots similar to the Shaner house but in much poorer condition, frame houses that leaned drunkenly on their foundations, rusted mobile homes and an occasional car or truck that made the ancient heap she drove look fancy by comparison.

They passed one man sitting on his front porch cleaning his day's kill—a couple of opossums. A little farther, they saw two teenage girls standing by the side of a creek simultaneously smoking cigarettes and fishing.

Several mongrel dogs darted in front of them or chased the truck, most of them with a suspicious resemblance to one another.

All of this Zach took in with his sharp, watchful eyes, but he remained silent.

Ellie decided he ought to meet his closest neighbor. So the last stop they made before returning to the ranch was Ben Poteet's. As they bumped down his rutted driveway, the old man was carrying a small bale of hay toward a muddy pasture, where a half-dozen doleful-eyed Hereford cattle lined the fence, waiting for supper.

"I suppose Mr. Poteet won't like me, either," Zach said dryly as they climbed out of the truck.

"Probably not, but don't worry. Ben doesn't like anyone."

Zach was hardly comforted.

Ben Poteet was a robust-looking, snowy-haired man with a ruddy face, a bulbous nose and tobacco-stained teeth. He nodded toward his visitors, then continued on with his task, silently acknowledging that he'd seen them and would deal with them as soon as it was convenient.

Meanwhile Zach took in the state of Poteet's frame house. It was in much better shape than the homes of some of his neighbors, but the house was still a shambles by Zach's St.

Louis standards. These people lived in one of the most naturally beautiful spots in the country, yet the poverty in Rocky Ridge was appalling.

"'Afternoon, Miss Ellie," Ben greeted them once his cattle were contentedly munching hay. Then he eyed Zach speculatively. "And you must be young Shaner, ol' Clem's nephew. Nice little spread you fell into."

"It's nice, all right," Zach agreed blandly, although he could have argued the point.

"What're you all slicked up for?" Ben asked pointedly.

Zach had already figured out that the people around here were more casual about business attire than he was used to. He'd been the only man wearing a tie in Rosie's Café, and he'd garnered his share of stares. "I had a meeting in Ledbetter with a representative from SunnyLand," he replied, seeing no point in being evasive.

"Hmmph," Ben said, hitching his thumbs into the pockets of his dusty overalls. "You gonna sell?"

"I don't know yet."

"Clem sure didn't want to sell. But then, Clem was an ornery old cuss. Sometimes I think he was holding out just for the sake of bein' contrary."

"Oh, now, Ben, you know that's not true," Ellie put in.

Ben shook his head. "Well, now, I'm not so sure. Clem would have been set for life with the money them developers offered. He coulda retired in style."

"Are you in favor of the theme park, then?" Zach asked.

"Hell, no! Bunch of city folks, lousing up the hills with their bulldozers and road pavers, bringin' in crowds and traffic and noise, stinkin' up the air." He waved his hand in dismissal. "You can have the bunch of 'em. 'Course, I understand you gotta do what you gotta do." The disapproval evident in the furrowed lines of his forehead belied the sentiment.

"The SunnyLand people say they'll invest money in Rocky Ridge and the other communities around the park," Zach pointed out. "What if there were low-interest money available for, say, home improvement?"

"You sayin' there's something wrong with my house, boy?"

"No, no." Zach quickly backpedaled. "But say you wanted to put in a bathroom or a carport, or maybe add to your livestock, something like that. Would you think about applying for a loan?"

Ben scratched his head and squinted into the afternoon sun. "I ain't never had a debt in my life, and I ain't aimin to start now. 'Sides, you think any person in his right mind would loan money to a seventy-three-year-old man with a bad heart?" He shook his head. "Lot of nonsense."

Zach chanced a look at Ellie. She was smiling triumphantly. He was beginning to understand why she'd taken him on this little tour.

"Speaking of livestock," Ben said, his eyes lighting up a bit, "how're them ugly birds of yours, Ellie? I'm getting tired of waitin' for my egg."

"We're just entering the breeding season," Ellie explained, her words sounding a bit shopworn. She'd probably been asked that question one too many times. "Should be a couple more weeks at the most."

"Hmmph. Could have sworn you said that a couple weeks ago. And anyway, I think I should get a discount or something, seeing as how some of those devilish critters are grazing on *my* land."

"Your land?" Zach asked politely.

"Your thievin' uncle went and fenced in an acre of my land. I shoulda sued him for it years ago. At least if you sell to those developers, there'll be a new survey done."

"If I sell to SunnyLand, I will personally make sure that acre is deeded to you," Zach said.

Ben's only reaction to what Zach thought was a rather open-minded gesture was to scowl. "I got work to do," he said, abruptly turning on his heel.

"What's his problem?" Zach asked Ellie as they walked back to the truck.

Ellie smiled indulgently. "Oh, Zach, you just don't get it, do you? He was deliberately trying to pick a fight with you, and you went and said something nice. That's not how the game's played."

"Huh?"

"Ever since Clem died, Ben hasn't had anybody to argue with. They used to go on for hours about that stupid acre. I think he was hoping you would take up where Clem left off."

"Oh, I understand." But he wasn't sure he did.

They rode the rest of the way to the ranch in a contemplative silence. Zach was beginning to see that the simple business decision he'd planned to make wasn't so simple anymore. He was dealing with a whole different culture here, and it wasn't based on making a fast buck. Priorities were different. Quality of life was judged by a different scale. And he felt woefully unprepared to decide what was good for the community and what wasn't.

After Ellie parked the truck and they got out, she motioned for Zach to follow her. "There's another part of the Red Canyon you have to see," she said as she walked around to the back of the house.

The sound of running water grew louder, and soon Zach saw the source. There was a steep drop-off behind the house, below which was a creek, its liquid-silver waters tripping and bouncing off rocks that tried to block its descent.

"The Red Canyon Creek," Ellie explained as she brushed the dirt off a flat rock and sat down. "That's how the ranch got its name, even though we're in more of a valley than a canyon. Clem used to call this creek his own little slice of heaven.''

''I can see why.'' Not only was it pretty, but there was a certain peacefulness here, Zach thought, as he found his own perch on another rock, unmindful of getting his suit dirty.

Soon he found his gaze straying from the view of the creek, however, to take in Ellie's own unearthly beauty. As she sat quietly staring down at the crystal waters, the serenity in her expression made him want to touch her, to capture some of her inner calmness for himself.

He had never experienced true serenity in his own life. There had been satisfaction, certainly, derived from his success and the approval of his peers. But not that inner peace, the kind that could make a woman look like an angel.

She really did love this place. If there were any way to preserve it—any *sensible* way, he amended—he would do it in a heartbeat. He hated the fact that he was upsetting her life this way.

''Why was it important that you show me this now?''

She smiled wistfully. ''In case you haven't noticed, I'm using every tool in my limited arsenal to convince you not to sell.''

''But, Ellie...''

''We're so close, Zach! As soon as the hens start laying, it'll make a big difference. I've already got a willing buyer lined up for the eggs—Duane Scoggins, a rancher down in Texas. Prices are holding. If I just had a little more time, I could—''

''How much time?'' He couldn't believe he was even entertaining the idea.

She grabbed at the sheer fabric of hope he'd woven with those three little words. ''One week,'' she answered decisively. ''Or two, maybe two at the most.''

"But even when you start collecting eggs, you'll have to sell them and pay off your investors. What does that leave for the ranch?"

"If I can get the shareholders to reinvest their egg proceeds—and I know I can convince them—it'll be like a shot in the arm. Besides, every third egg belongs to the ranch. We can start hatching chicks and selling them to the people around here to raise. As poor as they are, most of the Rocky Ridge residents have enough room and money to house a pair or two. Imagine, people who have lived their whole lives on public assistance using their own profits from the ostriches to make home improvements, rather than borrowing money from SunnyLand. Why, it would be almost like a miracle!"

Zach couldn't help but smile. He could easily see how her enthusiasm had caught the community's imagination. "Aren't you counting your ostriches before they hatch?"

She crossed her arms indignantly and asked through gritted teeth, "Are you being deliberately blind to the possibilities?"

"No. I understand what you're saying."

She peered at him from the corner of her eye. "So how'm I doing?" she asked with an unconsciously coquettish tilt of her head.

In all honesty her argument was at least two steps ahead of his objections. Or maybe it was just her. She was damn hard to say no to.

"You can have your two weeks," he said, so softly he barely heard his own words. He could hardly believe he'd said them. He was letting emotion get in the way of common sense, something he never would have done in his hard-hitting, high-rolling world back home. His father would have laughed in his face for being a soft touch. But dammit, Ellie had gotten under his skin with her crazy dream.

"What did you just say?" Her eyes were as round as silver dollars.

He stood decisively. "I said I'll give you two weeks. I think I can put off SunnyLand for that long. If, during that time, you can demonstrate—"

"Oh, thank you, Zach!" Before he knew what was happening she had sprung off her rock and launched herself at him in a showy but obviously heartfelt display of gratitude. She threw her arms around his neck and very nearly toppled him to the ground. "Thank you so much," she said again, her warm breath tickling his ear. "You won't regret it, I promise."

It was more than he could bear, this bundle of sensual energy pulsating down the length of his body. His arms wrapped themselves around her slender form. She felt incredibly fragile, like he could break her with one good squeeze, but she had shown him she was stronger than that.

They stood together like that for several suspended seconds as Zach's mind reeled with possibilities. Even as he acknowledged how ridiculous this was, he was conscious of Ellie's shallow, rapid breathing and the way her hands fluttered against his shoulder blades like frightened birds. He sensed her awareness, and an unlooked-for, unplanned cord of desire twined itself around them and through them.

She was all softness against his hardness, pliant as warm honey in his arms. He cocked his head back, saw the haze of longing that clouded her eyes, the expectation suggested by her parted lips, the hunger. And without a second thought he pressed his mouth against hers.

She tasted of life itself, and all he could think about was drinking until he was sated. He filled his senses with the softness of her moist lips against his, the delicate, flowery fragrance of her hair mixed with the fresh country air, the cottony feel of her much-washed shirt beneath his hands, warmed by the firm flesh underneath. He even welcomed the exquisite torture of her hips pressed against his rigid arousal.

No other woman had ever inflamed him so quickly, so completely. And if he didn't stop this right now...

Thankfully he didn't have to rely on his tenuous self-control. Ellie ended the kiss by bracing her hands on his shoulders and pushing herself away.

He was almost afraid to look at her. What would he see in those sincere blue eyes of hers—censure? Fear? But when he focused on her, he saw only a poignant wistfulness and maybe a little regret. She straightened his collar, her fingertips brushing impersonally against his neck, then stepped away from him.

"Er, I didn't mean to be that grateful," she said, looking anywhere but at him. "Sometimes I don't think before I ... well, I hope you won't take my enthusiasm the wrong way."

With his blood still singing through his veins, Zach resisted the urge to haul her against him and kiss her again. Instead he grinned at her. "I couldn't possibly take a kiss like that the wrong way."

She shook her head, now deadly serious. "What I mean is that—"

"I know what you mean, Ellie," he said, no longer teasing. "I'm giving you two weeks. In return, I don't expect anything."

She let out her breath in a relieved gust, then smiled tentatively, though still not meeting his gaze. She tucked a stray lock of her shiny brown hair behind her ear. "Good. I think I'll go get the mail. I forgot to check the box on the way in."

He watched her go, her hips swinging in that unconsciously provocative way of hers, still wondering how he had allowed that kiss to happen—and if he wanted it to happen again.

Ellie walked with the speed and sharp movements of a soldier on review. But she would have to go for miles and

miles before she could walk off her body's reaction to
Zach's kiss. Her heart pounded, her face felt flushed and
her mouth watered even as she tried to forget the taste of
him.

She hadn't meant for it to happen. Her joy at being given
a reprieve of two weeks had overcome her, resulting in that
spontaneous hug. But once she'd pressed up against him and
received the full force of his blatantly masculine self, it was
as if her free will had been whipped away by the wind. She'd
wanted to experience the taste and smell and feel of him.
And when she saw the matching hunger in his eyes, she had
simply let it all happen.

Thank goodness she'd found the presence of mind to pull
back before she'd been completely carried away. And thank
goodness he'd seen the impromptu embrace for what it
was—a show of gratitude that had gotten out of hand.
Given the timing, she wouldn't have blamed him if he'd
thought she was offering sex in return for his patience and
cooperation with the ranch.

She had no doubt Phyllis Quincy would eventually dan-
gle similar bait in front of Zach's nose if he didn't accept
SunnyLand's offer. The very idea made Ellie want to hy-
perventilate. She couldn't possibly compete with the glamorous and wealthy Ms. Quincy. But she wouldn't have to,
she reminded herself. Zach had more integrity than that.

By the time she reached the mailbox, she was feeling a bit
more normal—until she saw the red envelope from the
electric company. A disconnect notice. Her stomach sank.

She'd seen such notices before. She had approximately
five days to come up with more than a hundred and fifty
dollars, and her bank account was overdrawn. In fact, the
only cash she had was Bessie's ten-dollar bill.

Could she sell enough egg shares in the next few days to
make up the difference? The earliest investors had yet to see

any profits, and that made others reluctant. And she couldn't blame them. A few were beginning to look at her like she was a snake-oil peddler.

When she returned to the house, she found Zach in the kitchen, dressed once again in jeans, paired this time with a St. Louis Symphony T-shirt. She'd managed to forget that kiss for all of about a minute, but now the full force of his sexual appeal hit her in the face like a blast furnace. While a business suit made him look dashing and successful, she liked him in jeans. With a few good washings, those blue denims would fade and soften and mold themselves to his—

"Something wrong?"

She realized she was staring. "Uh, the electric bill," she said, improvising. "It always puts me in a bad mood."

"Oh. Well, I hate to trouble you, but will you have time to drive me to the airport? If we leave soon, I'll have plenty of daylight to—"

"You're leaving?" She winced at the hysterical note in her voice.

"Well, yeah. You've got work to do, and I'd just be in the way. Besides, I have my own company to manage. I postponed some important business to fly down here."

Of course he couldn't stay indefinitely, she chided herself. "I see."

"Under the circumstances, I thought you'd want me to leave."

"What circumstances?"

"You know." He cleared his throat. "Enthusiasm."

"Oh, that." She waved away his reason.

"Oh, *that?*" he repeated, bracing his fists on his hips. "Well, I must have made some impression on you."

She hadn't meant to wound the delicate male ego. "You did, but that's not the point."

"Then what is the point?"

"The point is..." She forced herself to get back to the matter at hand, which was saving the ostrich operation. "The point is, I was too optimistic. I need more than two weeks."

His expression hardened. "How much more time do you need?"

"Not more time, more money. They're gonna shut off my electricity, and frankly I don't feel right about selling more egg shares, now that there's a real possibility you'll sell the ranch and the shares will be worthless."

"How much money?" he asked cautiously.

"A hundred and fifty dollars."

He nodded, appearing decidedly relieved. "Hell, I should have realized. Tell you what. Before I go, I'll sit down and write out checks for all the outstanding bills. I think I can handle at least the most pressing debts. And they are my responsibility, after all."

The tightness in her chest eased as relief seeped clear to her bones. "Thanks, that'll be a big help. But..."

"Now what's wrong?" he asked, a trifle impatiently.

"Could you throw in a little extra for day help? If I'm going to get those birds laying eggs, I have a lot of work to do. I can hire my little brother for a few hours after school—he works cheap."

"I suppose that can be arranged. But look, Ellie, I have no intention of throwing my money down a black hole. My cash resources are limited, at least for the next year. All the money I've made has been poured into my finance company in St. Louis."

"I understand," she said primly. "I can assure you I've never spent a penny here that wasn't absolutely necessary.... What happens in a year?"

"I turn thirty. That's when I get control of the trust fund my father left for me. He didn't let me have it any earlier because he wanted me to have the satisfaction of making my own success first.''

"You don't sound the least bit disappointed," she observed.

"I'm not. He was right. He died when I was twenty-three, and I thought I knew everything. If I'd inherited a million-plus dollars then, I would've sat on my butt and never done anything with my life. Instead I've worked hard to get where I am, and I can be proud."

"A million?" she squeaked. That was almost twice what this entire spread was worth. It was such an awful lot of money. She was ashamed of herself for coveting that trust fund.

"Two million, counting the interest," he said with a shrug. "But not for another year, so it doesn't help us out now."

Us. She liked the sound of that. It indicated that Zach took his responsibility to the ranch seriously. Still, she forced herself to say, "Even if you did have control of it now, I wouldn't want you to dump your legacy from your father into such a risky operation."

"Risky? A few minutes ago you were telling me ostriches were almost as good as pure gold." He softened the remark with a wink.

"Oh, and I meant it, too... at the time. I find myself jumping from optimism to despair and back again with painful regularity," she said, shaking the electric bill she still clutched in her hand.

He glanced at his watch, then back at her. "It might take some time to get the finances straightened out," he said. "And I thought I would buy a pair of cowboy boots as long as I'm here, as a souvenir, you know. So I guess I can stay one more day—provided you let me cook dinner."

"Deal!" she agreed quickly as her heart gave a little leap. She wondered why she was so pleased at the prospect of having this city slicker around for another twenty-four hours. She feared it had little to do with the ranch's welfare and more to do with her.

Five

―――

"So, tell me about this urgent work that needs to be done," Zach asked the next morning. It was Saturday, and he sat with Ellie at the big kitchen table enjoying a country breakfast of eggs, sausage and biscuits. Zach had politely declined the sausage, fearing what it might contain. "Is it something I can help with?"

Ellie, her eyes still sexy and heavy lidded from sleep, took a sip of her coffee before answering. "Now that I've emptied your bank account, I thought you'd want to leave first thing," she said, referring to the previous evening's check-writing frenzy, during which Zach had paid out hundreds of dollars to the ranch's most anxious creditors. Her voice still had its early-morning raspiness, and it tickled his nerve endings.

"You didn't bankrupt me," he objected. Not yet, anyway. "And I changed my mind about rushing off. Last night I talked to Jeff Hodges, my second in command in St.

Louis. He said there's no urgent business that can't wait until Monday, so I thought I might stick around until tomorrow afternoon." He tossed this out casually.

"Oh, really?" Ellie's politely arched eyebrows indicated mild surprise, nothing more.

Funny, he'd gotten the impression that she'd *wanted* him to stay and take some responsibility for his inheritance. "You don't mind, do you?"

"No, I don't mind."

"Good. I'll be able to tie up any loose ends here and still have time to buy cowboy boots. There is someplace to buy boots, isn't there?"

She nodded, causing her unruly bangs to bob up and down. "Do you want them custom fitted? There's an excellent boot maker in Jasper, about an hour's drive from here."

Zach shook his head. Although the idea of custom boots had a certain appeal, he couldn't see forking over hundreds of dollars for something so frivolous when Ellie was living hand to mouth. "Boots off the rack should serve."

She smiled mischievously. "You could buy ostrich-leather boots. They're expensive, but kind of appropriate."

"I'll settle for plain cowhide, thanks." He shifted his feet under the table, accidentally brushing against her leg. They both pulled their feet back self-consciously, but the brief contact was surprisingly stimulating.

Everything about Ellie Kessler was stimulating, as a matter of fact, although she was nothing like the women who usually caught his attention. She wore no cosmetics; she didn't need them. Her peaches-and-cream skin, kissed golden by the sun, radiated a healthy glow that couldn't be improved upon. Her wardrobe leaned toward cotton rather than silk, but he was cultivating a new appreciation for simple, casual clothing—on her, anyway. The way those worn jeans clung to her slender thighs and cupped her bottom, they looked better on her than a designer evening gown might on another woman.

She wore her hair simply, either straight and loose to her shoulders or pulled back in a ponytail, but that only served to make it more touchable. If he ran his fingers through it, Ellie wasn't likely to complain that he was mussing it up— although she would probably object on other grounds.

She most assuredly did not flirt, as did so many of the other women he knew. Yet her every graceful gesture was mesmerizing. Ever since that unexpected kiss, he hadn't been able to get her off his mind. He kept wondering if she would welcome a repeat performance.

The whole notion of an involvement between them was ridiculous, he told himself. They were from completely different worlds. What would a businessman like himself and a little hillbilly girl have in common—other than an almost palpable physical attraction?

"You were asking about the work," she said, calling him back to their conversation. "What I need to accomplish today is some bird wrangling. Clem and I built special breeding pens on the back of the barn, and I need to transfer some of the mature birds into them. I was going to wait until I was sure they were ready, but—"

"How would you know?"

"Well, the males start showing an interest in the females, if you know what I mean."

"Oh."

"But on second thought, they'll be more manageable now, before the males get too aggressive. And maybe, once they're secluded in their own little love nests, they'll be more inclined to mate."

"This is a delicate matter, I take it."

"Oh, yes. Conditions have to be just right for them to breed. A pair or trio has to be compatible. Raising them together from chicks is the best way. And even then, you can't be sure they'll mate and produce offspring. That's why a proven pair is worth more money."

"And none of your...of our birds are proven yet, is that it?"

"Unfortunately. And they're *your* birds," she reminded him.

Zach tossed his napkin onto the table and leaned back in his chair. He was stuffed to the gills. He couldn't remember ever eating this well, even as a kid.

Not that his mother hadn't been an exemplary cook, but she had leaned toward fancier fare—exotic ingredients, elaborate presentations and small portions. She'd probably known how to cook like Ellie, he mused, but apparently she'd left those hearty Southern recipes behind along with the poverty.

"How exactly do you 'bird wrangle'?" he asked Ellie.

She tugged at her lower lip with her teeth, apparently trying to figure out how to explain the process. "Well, it's a challenge. You have to be part sheepdog and part bullfighter to do it."

"Is it dangerous?" He was actually more concerned for her than himself. Most of those ostriches were bigger than she was, and he hadn't forgotten what she'd told him about the razor-sharp toes.

She shrugged. "Nah. I've raised these guys from babies. The process of herding them into a trailer is more frustrating than dangerous."

He understood what she meant a short time later. They had hooked a horse trailer to the truck and backed it up to the gate that led to the ostrich pasture. Now, armed with empty feed bags to use as "matador's capes," they were attempting to cut one of the dun-colored females from the peacefully milling herd and maneuver her toward the trailer.

"How can you tell one from another?" Zach asked as they slowly edged their quarry toward the fence.

"They're banded. But I don't need to look at the bands. I can tell all eighteen apart. It's like I'm their mother. Whoa, girl," Ellie said to the bird as it tried to get around her. Her slow, honeyed voice had more effect on Zach than on the ostrich hen.

After several false starts, they managed to herd the hen into the trailer, where a bucket of feed pellets held her interest.

Ellie sighed. "Now for the second hen. I'm betting that once his two lady friends are corralled, the rooster will follow them." But she looked worried.

It occurred to Zach that this part of the operation was new to her. Until now, she'd been dealing with chicks. She didn't seem to be quite sure how these mature birds she had raised would react.

"So these birds are kind of kinky, huh?" he asked. "Two girls and one guy."

She rewarded him with a laugh. "It's not kinky, it's good business. One rooster can easily service two hens, and if you raise all three together, they don't seem to mind."

"Interesting arrangement." But not for Zach. He preferred one woman at a time, and right now he would prefer the woman to be Ellie Kessler. He couldn't keep his eyes off her, to the detriment of his matador duties.

The second hen went right into the trailer, and Ellie felt a burst of confidence. She hadn't moved the birds around at all since Clem's death because there hadn't been any need. This was the first time she'd attempted "bird wrangling" without him. But it wasn't so hard. At least, not yet. Now came the tough part.

"There's the rooster we need," she said, pointing to the biggest bird in the pasture. He stood darn near eight feet tall, with magnificent black-and-white plumage. He puffed up his feathers and flapped his wings as he strutted around, having clearly figured out that something was wrong.

"I'd be upset too, bud, if somebody took off with my woman," Zach commiserated with the ostrich.

Ellie smiled weakly. She would have a much better sense of humor about this once the big guy was in the trailer. "If he starts coming at you, just wave the bag in his face," she said. "They hate to have anything near their heads."

Just as she'd feared, the showy rooster resisted all efforts to corral him. Ellie and Zach would cut him out of the crowd, urging him along by talking and waving their feed bags. Then, just when he looked as though he might cooperate, he would dart to the side and run for the opposite corner.

"Damn, look at him go," Zach said.

Ellie sighed. "I guess we move to Plan B."

"I'm almost afraid to ask. What's Plan B?"

"We do like we did before, but just before he bolts, I grab him by the wings and guide him into the trailer."

Zach's face registered amusement, then patent disbelief. "You're kidding."

"No, that's how it's done." Usually by large, fearless men, but she didn't tell him that part. "I've watched it a zillion times. I think I can do it."

"Whatever you say. Let's round him up."

The plan went according to schedule until it came time for Ellie to grab the bird. At an opportune moment she pounced, wrapping her hands around base of his wings. He turned around and looked at her. She dug in her heels, determined not to lose her grip. Then he calmly flapped a couple of times and lurched out of her grasp. She fell bottom first onto the hard-packed ground, and the ornery bird left her quite literally in the dust.

She heard a snort of laughter from Zach's direction before he wisely stifled it. "Are you hurt?" he asked as he strode toward her.

"Just my pride." She took the hand he proffered and levered herself to her feet, allowing their palms to remain touching for a heartbeat longer than was necessary. She wished, sometimes, that she had prettier hands. Although nicely shaped, hers were callused and scarred from years of hard work, with blunt, practical nails.

She looked away from Zach and busily brushed the dirt off her jeans, chiding herself for being so vain at a time like this.

She'd been alone too much, that's all it was. For three years she'd been too busy with the Red Canyon to even think about men, much less kiss one. Zach Shaner had accidentally reawakened her hormones. Thank goodness he would soon be gone, and she wouldn't have to worry about it anymore.

"Your technique looked pretty good," Zach observed dryly, "but that bird out-muscled you. Maybe I should give it a try."

"You?" She managed to refrain from laughing. Oh, he had the muscles, all right. He probably had a health club in his office building where he dutifully pumped iron three times a week. But the idea of him wrestling with an ostrich...

"Yes, me," he said indignantly. "I think I can do it."

Far be it from her to interfere with the delicate male ego. "Be my guest," she said. "Just be sure to grab him at the base of the wing, not farther out, so you don't injure him."

The male ostrich had calmed down, so Ellie and Zach went through the now-familiar herding procedure. When the bird became suddenly alert to the fact that he was being trapped, Zach made his move. Amazingly, he held on to the surprised rooster, and they more or less dragged each other to the mouth of the trailer, raising a cloud of dust.

When the dust cleared, the bird was in the trailer with his mates and Zach was triumphantly closing the tailgate—mi-

nus his loafers, which had been left behind during the scuf-
fle.

"Well done!" Ellie congratulated him. She looked down
at his socks. "But you definitely do need some boots."

Zach was grinning ear to ear. "You might make a bird
rancher out of me yet."

Ellie found herself fervently hoping he was right. She had
missed Clem. She didn't like running the ranch by herself.
But she was deluding herself if she thought this was anything more than a lark for Zach.

They drove the trailer to one of the breeding pens attached to the back of the barn. Each pen had a smooth sand
floor, a water trough, a food bowl and a door leading into
a small enclosure inside the barn, for inclement weather.
Inside the shelter was a fake nest holding a decoy egg, to
encourage laying, Ellie explained.

The trio of birds exited the trailer easily enough, blinked
their big, long-lashed eyes at their new surroundings, then
calmly began pecking at the sand, apparently no worse for
wear.

"No one ever claimed they have brains," Ellie said.

"What next?"

"Back to the pasture. We have another trio and a duo to
put in the pens. The rest of the birds are too young to
breed."

Zach frowned, but he didn't complain openly.

Ellie hid a smile. He'd probably had no idea what he was
letting himself in for when he'd volunteered to help with the
work, but he was handling it admirably.

The other birds were more cooperative than the first trio.
Either that or Ellie and Zach were getting better at herding
them. But it was still afternoon when they were done.

Ellie heaved a sigh of relief as the last two ostriches were
put into their pen. "I'd say this calls for a celebration. What

do you say we have some grilled cheese sandwiches for lunch, then go into town and buy you some boots?''

"Lady, you're on!"

She returned his grin, feeling suddenly giddy and carefree. She'd been dreading this business of moving the birds more than she realized. Now that it was over, she wanted to kick up her heels. She didn't even object when Zach threw his arm around her shoulders as they walked back to the house. The gesture seemed as natural as breathing.

Working together and accomplishing a challenging task had forged a tenuous bond between them, Ellie supposed. She was actually starting to like him, even if he did pose a threat to the future she envisioned. He had more grit and fair-mindedness than she had at first thought. But then, he was Clem's kin. He must have something of his uncle in him.

Zach was immediately taken with Bootlegger, the leather-goods shop in town. The deep, narrow store, with its wood plank flooring and rattling ceiling fans, boasted a wide selection of leather footwear in all price ranges as well as saddles, bridles, belts, purses, wallets and anything else Zach could imagine being made of animal hide. The rich scent of leather filled every corner of the place.

Ellie introduced Zach to the ancient proprietor, a stooped man named Dan with a long, gray beard who resembled Rip van Winkle himself. Dan was helpful but not pushy. When Zach, with Ellie's reserved counsel, finally selected three styles to try on, the old man zipped to the back room with more spryness than seemed possible.

"I like the lizard skin ones best," Ellie said.

Zach did, too. But they were a hundred dollars more than either of the calfskin styles, and he felt uncomfortable at the idea of spending that kind of money in front of Ellie, considering her impossibly tight budget. On the other hand she

had staunchly refused when Zach had offered to pay her at
least part of her back salary. She'd insisted that the Red
Canyon had been supporting her adequately all these
months, and that no additional payment was necessary.

As they waited for the old man to reappear, Ellie wan-
dered over to inspect a pair of ladies' boots. They were made
of buff-colored suede and sported lots of fancy stitching.
She caressed the soft leather with her fingertips as she
looked at the boots with what could only be considered
longing.

Her expression stole the breath right out of Zach's lungs.
He could imagine her looking at *him* that way. "Why don't
you try those on?" he suggested.

She jumped. "Hmm? Oh, these." She set the boot down
guiltily, then looked down at her own boots, which were so
worn Zach couldn't discern the original color. "No, I don't
think so,' she said, dragging out the words. "These old
boots of mine have at least another year left in 'em. Anyway, if I were to buy boots, I'd choose something a little
more practical than these." But she again picked up one of
the suede boots and stroked it.

"Why don't you try them on for fun, then?" Just then the
old man reappeared and set three large boxes down by
Zach's chair. "Could you show the lady a pair of those
cream-colored boots in her size, please?" Zach asked.

"Surely. Just got those in yesterday. What size do you
wear, Ellie?"

"Ah..." Zach watched her fight with temptation and
lose. "Seven, I guess."

Zach quickly tried on all three pairs Dan had brought out,
but he knew almost immediately which ones he wanted. The
lizard-skin boots fit like they'd been made for his feet. They
were much more comfortable than either of the other two
pairs.

"Sharp," Ellie commented as her eyes caressed him as surely as her fingers now absently caressed the boot she held. "You could wear those to church."

"I don't know. Once I get home, I might feel funny about wearing them." And where would they be appropriate, come to think of it? Not at work. Not to socialize. On weekends, maybe, at home.

Ellie shrugged. "I can't imagine owning a pair of boots like that and not wearing them, but it's up to you."

Ah, hell. There was really no question. He would take the damn lizard-skin ones.

The proprietor reappeared with the boots for Ellie. She dutifully tried them on, admired them in the mirror, then pranced around the store a bit, much to Zach's delight.

"Those look mighty pretty on you, Ellie," the old man said as he checked the fit.

"Mmm-hmm." She sighed and flopped down into her chair. "But not this year. Pull 'em off, Dan."

He did as she asked. "Any eggs yet?"

Ellie brightened. "No, but we just put some birds in the breeding pens today. Another week or two at the most."

"Good, good. M'wife's gettin' kinda antsy about the investment we made."

"Don't worry," Zach said. "You'll get your money back, I can promise you that."

Ellie shot him a grateful look.

As he took out his credit card to pay for his purchase, Zach whispered to the old man, "Slip those boots Ellie tried on into the sack, too."

Dan nodded and winked.

They stopped at the grocery store on the way home, where Ellie protested as Zach filled a basket with enough food for a month's worth of meals. He refused to let her continue subsisting on the questionable fare from her pitiful freezer. He even bought her a supply of shampoo, soap and toothpaste, having noticed when he used her bathroom that she was almost out of everything.

"I don't like taking your charity," she grumbled as they stood in line at the single checkout.

"Ellie, honey, it's not charity. The Red Canyon *owes* you. *I* owe you, for taking care of the place for me. You weren't obligated to stay after Clem died. If you hadn't, I shudder to think what a mess the place would be in. Furthermore, if you need anything during the next two weeks, I want you to call me in St. Louis."

"I'm sure everything will be fine," she murmured.

True to his word, Zach made dinner that night. Ellie watched him with growing appreciation as he moved around the kitchen with relative ease. He even tackled the wood-burning range with aplomb, and soon had a mouth-watering beef stir-fry served up on a platter, brimming with broccoli, peppers and water chestnuts.

Her mouth watered as the tantalizing aroma filled her nose. "Where on earth did you learn to cook like this?" she asked as she eagerly heaped a ladleful of the concoction over a bed of rice.

"Same as you, from watching my mom. I remember when I was a kid she always had her nose stuck in some gourmet magazine or cookbook. Chinese stir-frying was one of the first things she mastered. It's really easy."

"And a sight more healthy than the heavy fried foods I cook," Ellie said before popping a bit into her mouth. Mmm, heaven. "You know, if you stuck around here for very long, you'd have every single girl in the county chasing after you. A husband who cooks is a rarity around here."

She immediately regretted her quip. She'd intended that it be amusing, but what if he thought she was making a play for him? She couldn't blame him, not after the way she'd thrown herself into his arms the day before.

Fortunately he took the teasing in stride. "Well, it's a good thing I'm not sticking around, then," he said. "'Cause I'm not planning to take on a wife anytime soon."

"Why's that?" she asked, overcome by curiosity. She'd always thought that when a man achieved success, as Zach obviously had, the next step was to find a wife to enjoy it with him.

He shrugged. "I like my freedom too much."

Much as she tried to deny the disappointment, her heart sank. Not that she honestly thought there could be anything between them. That was patently ridiculous. But a freedom-loving man was less likely to hold on to a ranch than a homebody might be.

"Suppose I prove myself during the next few weeks," she said carefully, broaching the subject that had been eating at her.

He looked at her sharply, and she realized he still thought they were talking about marriage.

She quickly straightened him out. "What I mean is, suppose the *ranch* proves itself—the ostriches start laying eggs and the money starts coming in. What will you do?"

His expression grew thoughtful. "Sell it as a working entity, I imagine. Once you can prove there's a steady income, the property will be a much more practical investment. I probably won't find a buyer overnight, but with my connections in financial circles, I'm sure I can dig up someone with an avid interest in bird ranching and a bankroll to match."

Her disappointment expanded like air in a balloon until her chest felt full of it. "Are you sure you wouldn't like to keep it? I mean, the land's been in the Shaner family for generations, since before they opened the Oklahoma territory to white settlement, Clem told me. It'd be a shame to let it fall into a stranger's hands."

"Ellie," he said softly, "Clem never intended for me to have this estate. He and my father hadn't spoken for years, remember? Anyway, I have no business running a ranch. At best I would be a distracted, absentee owner. The Red Canyon needs someone who'll care for it and look after your interests, too. As a matter of fact—"

He paused, staring off into space. She could almost see the gears turning inside his head. When he looked at her again, it was with the light of inspiration in his green eyes. "I've got a great idea. Why don't *you* buy it?"

"Me?" She laughed uproariously. "With what?"

"With a year's worth of back salary, for starters."

She waved away his ridiculous suggestion. "That wouldn't be enough for a down payment."

"It would if I said it was. It's my ranch. I can structure the deal any way I please."

Her heart gave an uncomfortable little leap as she realized he was serious. Lord, she should be ecstatic. Clem had said to her more than once that he wanted the ranch to come to her when he died. And hadn't she been upset when she'd discovered he'd died without a will, and that some relative she'd never met had inherited?

But Zach's idea didn't thrill her at all. She didn't want to own the ranch by herself. Against all logic, she wanted Zach to care about this place the way his uncle had.

"You're forgetting something," she said softly. "The bank owns a significant portion of this spread. Any sale you propose would have to be approved by them. And I'm telling you, that sour-faced loan officer won't approve of *me*, seeing as how I've been late with every single payment since Clem died."

"Oh, you'd be surprised at the deals I can work out," Zach said. "At any rate, we don't have to make any decisions yet. Over the next two weeks I'll send out some feelers and see what kind of interest I can generate."

"Yeah. Sounds like a good idea." Ellie ate the rest of her dinner in silence, hardly tasting the food that had seemed so delicious a few minutes before.

On the way to the airstrip the following afternoon, Ellie kept up a steady stream of conversation, trying to mask the illogical letdown she felt at the thought of Zach's leaving.

She should be *glad* to see him go. Now she wouldn't have to worry about feeding him, entertaining him or sharing her bathroom. Although, come to think of it, the latter had some advantages. This morning she'd emerged from her bedroom just as he was walking out of the bathroom wrapped in nothing but a towel. They'd both murmured "Excuse me," and after an uncomfortable moment when their eyes had locked in awareness, he had nodded and sauntered down the hall. The sight of those terry-wrapped buns had just about done her in.

"And so what did she do?" Zach's question broke through her reverie.

"Uh, what?"

"What did your mother do when she caught your brother with a dozen baby chicks in his closet?"

Ellie realized she'd gotten so wrapped up in the memory of Zach's backside that she'd halted mid-story. "Well, she threatened to tan his hide, of course," she said, quickly picking up the threads of the familiar tale, "but she didn't when she saw how upset he was. That was the first time he realized that the chicken we ate for dinner was the very same as the chickens we raised in the coop. He was only four."

Zach laughed. "And how are you going to feel in a few years when the ostrich market matures and it becomes profitable to start butchering your very own birds?"

"I'll live," she said. "As a matter of fact, when that one emu was shot, Clem took it to a meat processor and had it turned into meatballs. Neither of us had ever tasted emu or ostrich meat before."

Zach grimaced. "And how was it?"

"Pretty yummy—like beef, sort of, only much healthier. It has less fat than even chicken. We passed it around the neighborhood so other folks could try it. Most people liked it."

"At least you got some public-relations use from the incident," he said.

"Yeah. I bet SunnyLand was ticked off when they found out."

"You don't really think SunnyLand was responsible for killing that bird, do you?"

"I certainly do."

There was a pause. "You'll be careful, living here by yourself, won't you?"

"I'll be fine." *And I wouldn't be by myself if you'd stick around and take responsibility for your ranch,* she thought, grousing inwardly. But she knew she was being unfair. She kept reminding herself that this inheritance had come out of the blue for Zach. He was dealing with it as best he knew how.

At the airstrip, Zach prepared his plane for the flight home as Ellie watched with interest. He offered to take her for a quick spin, but she declined. She didn't admit that, like the ostriches, she'd never flown before and had no intention of starting now.

He shook her hand just before climbing aboard. Then, as if realizing how impersonal the gesture was, he took one of her hands in both of his and squeezed it, then leaned down and kissed her cheek. The gesture sent her heart into a wild gallop.

Damn, but she wanted to feel his arms around her again. She made herself take a step back before she did something foolish.

"You remember to call me if you have any problems I can help with," he said sternly. Then his eyes sparkled, and he flashed a smile that made her go weak in the knees. "And I'll see you in two weeks."

She watched from a distance as Zach started up the engine. He taxied to the end of the runway, revved the engine to an ear-splitting scream and took off like a bullet, pulling off the ground just as the pavement ran out. The plane climbed sharply, barely topping the trees.

She watched until it was no more than a dot. Surely she would be too busy over the next two weeks to think about him.

She climbed into the truck and immediately spotted a cardboard box on the passenger seat. On the lid was hand-written No Arguments! With shaking hands she opened the box to reveal the buff-colored boots of butter-soft suede she had tried on at Bootlegger.

She felt like crying.

Six

"**Y**ou miserable sluggards," Ellie grumbled as she replenished a bucket of pellets in one of the breeding pens. "Just my luck, I managed to raise undersexed ostriches." The male, who by now should have been chasing his hens around on a regular basis and intolerant of a human presence invading his territory, calmly approached the bucket and began pecking down pellets.

She wanted to grab him around his scrawny pink neck and shake the complacency out of him. But she resisted. One thing she knew was that the birds wouldn't breed if they were upset or disturbed in any way.

"If I don't start seeing some action, I'm turning you all into meatballs," she warned—softly—as she exited the pen.

She saw to the other pens, quietly moving in and out with fresh feed and water. As she was about to enter the barn to put away the buckets, she noticed a cloud of dust at the entrance to the ranch.

"Great," she grumbled, quickly setting her supplies just inside the door. Here she was in her most disreputable clothes—overalls, of all things—and someone was coming to see her. She hadn't even had a cup of coffee yet.

She peered at the approaching vehicle, trying to get a clue as to who her morning caller might be. But the large, shiny blue, late-model American car wasn't at all familiar. No one around here drove a car that nice. She hoped it wasn't someone from SunnyLand. She was in no mood to deal with that witch Phyllis Quincy or any of her pushy cohorts.

Ellie grabbed a rusty pitchfork from the barn before going to meet the visitor. It never hurt to be prepared.

When she saw a familiar dark blond head emerge from the car, a dozen emotions hit her at once. *Zach!* What was he doing here? Her heart gave a happy skip at the sight of him as he stood staring at her, wearing a pair of stone-washed jeans, a Western shirt, the cut of which emphasized his wide shoulders, and his boots. All he needed was a Stetson hat to be the quintessential urban cowboy.

Stetson or no, he looked luscious.

Along with the perfectly irrational joy at seeing him again came a thread of panic. Tomorrow her two weeks would be up, and she didn't have one egg to show for it.

"What are you doing here?" she blurted out.

"It's nice to see you, too, Ellie."

She ran a hand over her face. "Sorry. You just surprised me, showing up this early. I'm all discombobulated."

He laughed. "You're all what?"

"Discombobulated. It means I'm flustered." She could feel the heat rising to her face. Her clothes were a mess, her eyes were still half-closed from sleep, and she hadn't even bothered to comb her hair. She'd been anxious to check on the ostriches, only to be disappointed again.

"Well, combobulate yourself and tell me what's been going on. I haven't heard a word from you."

She frowned. "Unfortunately there's been nothing to report. Want some coffee? I left a pot brewing in the kitchen."

"Mmm, I'd love some." He followed her into the cabin, where they were greeted by the smell of Ellie's hand-ground coffee. "I flew into Muskogee last night to meet with a prospective buyer."

"Oh." Ellie's stomach sank as she filled two cups with the strong, fragrant brew.

Zach pulled out one of the ladder-back chairs, but he never got around to sitting down. He was obviously excited about this new development, and he paced the kitchen as he continued his explanation. "This guy is a friend of a friend of a business acquaintance. He and his wife came all the way from California to look over the Red Canyon. They're getting ready to retire and are absolutely fascinated with the idea of ostrich farming. I know they have the financial backing to pay my asking price. They were especially impressed with the fact that the operation comes equipped with its own bird-ranching expert."

"I'm not a piece of equipment," Ellie objected as she slammed her cup down on the table, the hot contents sloshing over her fingers.

Zach stopped pacing. "Ellie, what's wrong? I thought you'd be pleased. If this guy comes through, he could be the answer to all our problems. He's got the time, the enthusiasm and the money to make this place a success, and SunnyLand can put its parking lot somewhere else."

Ellie slumped into a chair with a weary sigh. "I'm sorry, Zach. Of course you're right." Then why wasn't she excited about the prospect of Zach selling the Red Canyon? "I guess it's just the idea of an outsider coming in and taking over that bothers me."

"He's no more an outsider than I am," Zach pointed out.

"Yes, he is. You were born here. You have a connection. You're a Shaner, and you belong on Shaner land. This guy from California is—"

"Is really nice," Zach finished for her as he took her hand and tenderly dried it with a dish towel, then mopped up the coffee she'd spilled on the table. "He's coming out this afternoon to look the place over. That's why I rented a car and drove in from Muskogee so early. I wanted to give ourselves plenty of time to get everything ready." Finally he sat down.

"The only thing that's not ready is me," Ellie said, running her fingers through her mussed hair. "If I'm part of the bargain, I'd best go clean myself up." She took a fortifying gulp of coffee before setting the cup on the table and pushing back her chair. She felt a desperate need to get away by herself, where she could collect her thoughts and make herself presentable.

As she walked past Zach, he reached out and took hold of her arm, gently pulling her to a stop. His hand was warm and insistent as his fingers circled her slender wrist. His gaze traveled down her body until it reached her feet. "You're not wearing your new boots."

That was a whole different argument she wasn't equipped to deal with just now. "They're too pretty to work in," she murmured. "Those are dress-up boots."

"And where does one wear dress-up boots around these parts?"

She shrugged uncomfortably. "To church, I guess."

"There must be somewhere else. Does anyone go out dancing?"

"Sure. There's a country-and-western place on the edge of town called Hooper's."

"Suppose we go there tonight," he said. "Then we can both show off our new boots."

She smiled, for the first time in days, it seemed. "Okay."

He nodded and released her.

As she let the hot spray of the shower wash the morning fog from her mind, Ellie wondered why she'd agreed to go dancing with Zach. Gossip was already running rampant about the city slicker who'd inherited Clem Shaner's spread. A lot of people had seen him when he'd gone into town. Over the past two weeks, several men had pointedly inquired if Ellie needed any help handling him. And the women had slyly asked if he was as hot as he was hot looking.

If she showed up at Hooper's with him, in a new pair of boots that were obviously beyond her means, she would never still the wagging tongues.

Maybe that wasn't so bad. Most of her life no one had paid much attention to her. She'd always been plain little Ellie Kessler, the good girl, the one who went to college. More recently she'd been known as Ellie Kessler, the crazy ostrich lady. Maybe it wouldn't hurt her reputation to be connected with the dashing Zach Shaner.

But there was her heart to think of. Already she found it far too easy to succumb to Zach's sophisticated charm. And while she'd never considered herself fragile or easily hurt when it came to her emotions, Zach was in a unique position to hurt her badly. He held her whole future in the palm of his hand. She had no business being attracted to a man like that.

Zach refilled his coffee cup and marveled at what had just happened. He had asked a woman wearing overalls to go dancing with him—at a country-and-western bar. Furthermore, he was looking forward to it.

His attitude certainly had changed since his first trip to Rocky Ridge. This time, he'd actually found himself happily anticipating the visit. Rearranging his schedule hadn't been an inconvenience at all. A chocolate-haired, blue-eyed wisp of a woman with a voice like warm honey made all the difference in the world. He was unbearably attracted to her, and he wasn't quite sure what to do about it.

If she were someone he'd met in St. Louis, he would approach it with his usual style—some good times, no strings attached, and no tears when it ended. But Ellie seemed too damn wholesome for that sort of arrangement. Yet anything more was out of the question. Their contrasting lifestyles, not to mention the fact that they lived hundreds of miles apart, prohibited anything more permanent, even if he were of a mind to consider commitment—which he wasn't.

What, then, to do about her?

He was reasonably sure asking her to go dancing wasn't the answer. He needed to get this place sold and get the hell out, before his raging hormones got him into trouble.

When Ellie reappeared, surrounded by an aura of soap scent that reminded him of a fresh spring rain, her spirits were higher, her smile quicker, her eyes brighter. She had put on a pair of jeans slightly less disreputable than the overalls, matching them with a peach-colored oversize T-shirt. The shirt was soft and faded from many washings, and it draped invitingly over her small, rounded breasts.

Zach's mouth went dry.

"I feel a hundred percent more human," she declared. "I'm afraid you caught me at my worst. My folks say my wick's turned down real low until I've had my coffee and a shower. So, how about some breakfast? I can whip up some hotcakes in no time."

"That sounds terrific. But I don't want to keep you away from your work."

"There's nothing urgent that needs doing. All the birds except the emu have been fed and watered, although I'm sorely tempted to starve them. Maybe *that* would prompt them into some sort of productive activity."

"You mean they're not even . . . ?"

"I haven't caught them at it." She smiled mischievously, then paused with a slight frown, her teeth worrying her lower lip.

"Well, whatever needs doing, I'll help out. I want everything looking efficient when Mr. and Mrs. Forsythe get here this afternoon."

"Everything else is in good shape. In fact, yesterday I rearranged the barn and threw out some stuff. If you want to earn your keep, later you can help me with the garden."

"Sure thing."

Gardening. Normally the thought made him cringe. He could still remember weeding his mother's flower garden when he was a kid, and hating every moment of it even though he was getting paid. But the idea of kneeling side by side in the dirt with Ellie evoked a completely different feeling—warm sunshine, fertile earth, growing things....

After gorging on hotcakes swimming with butter and syrup, Zach allowed Ellie to guide him through the day the way the wind moves a cloud. They went to feed and water the emu, which were at the opposite end of the valley from the ostriches. Zach found these gray birds more likable than their larger cousins. Their long, thin feathers gave them a furry, almost cuddly look, and their temperaments seemed more docile. He even persuaded one of the birds to eat pellets out of his hand.

"Are these guys fully grown?" he asked.

"Some of them," Ellie replied. "The ones with the purplish bald spots on their heads and necks are more mature. They breed through the fall and winter, which dovetails nicely with the ostrich breeding season."

"That'll be a good selling point for Mr. Forsythe."

"Who?"

"Richard Forsythe, the buyer who's coming out this afternoon."

"Oh, him." She tossed an empty feed sack into the back of the truck. "Let's go. There's gardening to be done. Angie Kelso brought over the most beautiful tomato plants in exchange for—"

"Ellie! I thought you weren't going to sell any more egg shares."

"I didn't," she replied hotly. "This was a deal we made weeks ago. I could hardly renege now."

"Okay, okay, simmer down."

The storm clouds receded from her expression to be replaced by a delighted smile. "Simmer down?"

"I got the expression from you," he said defensively, appalled that he was picking up the local colloquialisms. His mother was probably spinning in her grave.

"And I got it from Clem. I'll swear, I see more and more of your uncle in you all the time."

Oh, no, she wasn't going to use that sentimental logic on him again. "I'm not keeping the ranch, Ellie."

She put her hands on her hips. "So you've said. I'm clear on that point. It was just an innocent observation, okay?"

"Okay. Where's the garden?"

They spent the next couple of hours contentedly digging holes, planting tomato plants and weeding the rest of the garden. It was an impressive vegetable patch, with neat rows of radishes, lettuce, peppers, squash, cucumbers, onions and potatoes. Zach could imagine the tasty salads Ellie would be making in a month or so. If the garden was still here. If it wasn't covered with blacktop.

The Forsythes, Richard and his wife, Eva, showed up a little after two. Zach could tell by the pinched expression on Eva's face that she didn't care for the house. As they took a tour of the ranch, with Ellie dutifully explaining how the operation worked and what she expected in the future, Eva's expression never wavered.

How could the woman fail to be moved? Zach wondered. Ellie spoke with such obvious love and devotion for her work that it brought a tightness to Zach's throat. If the Forsythes didn't buy, and he sold out to SunnyLand, where would she go? What would she do? How could he possibly force her to give up this life that meant so much to her?

After a ten-minute perusal of the Red Canyon's financial records, Richard stood decisively and shook his head. "I'm sorry, Zach, but I don't think this is the right property for us. I appreciate the time you've taken, and if in the course of business you run across something more, uh—"

"Something a little nicer," his wife put in.

"A ranch that's already, you know, going strong," Richard said. "That's more what we're looking for."

Zach nodded and promised to keep his eyes open, all the while squelching his disappointment. Then, sensing an impending explosion from Ellie, he quickly sent the couple on their way.

"Something nicer!" Ellie erupted before the Forsythes' car had even cleared the driveway. "Something *nicer?* What the hell do they think an ostrich farm is, a petting zoo? Do they think they're going to just waltz in to some fancy ostrich operation that's making money hand over fist and *buy* it? No one wants to sell a farm that's 'going strong,' as Mr. Forsythe put it."

She strode angrily into the house, slamming the door in Zach's face—probably not even aware he was behind her, he figured. He calmly opened it again and followed her inside, where he found her pacing and muttering.

"Those two idiots wouldn't know a good investment if it bit them on their fancy California fannies. Did you see the fingernails on that lady? She's probably never worked a day in her life. And she wants to own ostriches—hah! I'm glad they didn't want to buy the Red Canyon. They'd probably run it into the ground within a month."

Zach refrained from pointing out that the Red Canyon was already into the ground. In fact, he said nothing. He'd been counting on the Forsythes to at least think about making an offer. Now he was back where he'd started. Wealthy people who wanted to buy ostrich ranches didn't grow on trees. And any he managed to find would probably react just as the Forsythes had when they saw this place, which was something less than impressive looking.

He came up behind Ellie and put his hands on her shoulders, which trembled with the force of her anger. Only then did she stop her pacing and muttering, looking over her shoulder at him. She seemed surprised to find him there.

"Sorry," she said. "But it's not easy to watch while someone discounts three years of hard work, like it doesn't mean anything."

"I know. I appreciate what you've done here. I really do." And he had no idea how to show his appreciation. Selling the ranch to SunnyLand wasn't the way, but he was rapidly running out of options. He had a silly urge to lean down and plant a kiss on the tender flesh at the base of her neck—as if that would help. "How long has it been since you had a steak dinner with all the trimmings?" he asked, more to distract himself than her.

She whirled to face him, suddenly much too close. "Steak?" her blue eyes searched his face. "What does steak have to do with anything?"

"Nothing, except I thought it might put you in a better mood. I imagine you're pretty tired of cooking. I'll take you out to the fanciest place around here. And if there's not a fancy place, we'll drive all the way to Muskogee."

She blinked at him a couple of times. He could tell she liked the idea. "There's . . . there's a place on the lake," she said. "It's a tourist spot, the Choctaw Inn. Not all that fancy, but the food's wonderful. We wouldn't have to get all gussied up."

It occurred to him that she might not have anything to get "gussied up" with. If he thought he could get away with it, he'd take her out and buy her a ruffly, feminine dress. He would enjoy seeing her draped in something low-cut and off the shoulder, maybe with a bit of lace against her warm, golden skin. But there was no way she would agree to that, not after the way she'd fought him on those boots.

He ruffled her bangs, which were, as usual, already ruffled. "Let's do it. And then we can go dancing at that Hooper's place you told me about earlier. We'll forget all about Mr. and Mrs. Whosit and their stupid opinions."

"Okay," she said, still sounding a trifle uncertain, as if she wasn't quite sure of his motives but was unable to resist the temptation of an evening out. "I'll call and make reservations."

Zach poured himself some lemonade, watching Ellie from the corner of his eye as she made the telephone call. She was right to mistrust his motives. And he was crazy if he thought an expensive dinner would soften the blow when he pulled the rug out from under her life.

But that was what he was about to do. He had promised her two weeks, against his better judgment, and all she'd managed to accomplish was to get the ranch two weeks further into debt. Now that the Forsythes had gone running back to California, Zach had no choice but to sell to SunnyLand. Tomorrow, when Ellie's two weeks were officially over, he would tell her. And tonight, he thought guiltily, he would enjoy the harmony between them, artificial though it was. It was likely to be the last evening she would spare a kind word or thought for him.

Ellie dressed with exceptional care. Her wardrobe was sadly lacking, but she did have one outfit she particularly liked, a fitted denim dress with a row of fancy gold buttons down the front. She had bought it a couple of years ago, when Clem was paying her a salary, but the classic style still served. Underneath the dress she wore a lacy camisole.

She combed the front of her hair away from her face and fastened it at her crown with a beaded clip she'd won at Choctaw Bingo Night. Her bangs, as usual, went their own way, but there was nothing she could do about them. Nature had given her an odd assortment of cowlicks.

She even dug into her supply of carefully hoarded cosmetics, although she used very little—some mascara to brighten her eyes, a dusting of powder for her shiny nose, a dab of clear lip gloss. She wished she had some perfume, but that was a luxury she couldn't afford.

At last she pulled on the buff-colored boots. She hadn't yet worn them outside the privacy of her room, always intending to return them.

When she was finished, she inspected herself in the mirror. No matter how she tried to tell herself that she was primping simply because she wanted to look her best during a rare evening out, she knew that every bit of her careful preparations were for Zach's sake.

The whole thing was silly. What did she expect, that he would become so enamored with her gorgeous body that he wouldn't be able to tear himself away and return to St. Louis?

"Silly goose," she murmured to her reflection, using another of Clem's favorite expressions. She was behaving no better than a girl with a teenage crush. Nonetheless, as she walked out her bedroom door she unfastened the top two buttons on the dress to reveal a tiny bit of the lace beneath.

Her heart thumped like a conga drum as she entered the kitchen and Zach issued a low whistle of appreciation.

"You look gorgeous, Ellie." A light of sincere approval burned in his eyes.

"Thank you," she murmured, unaccustomed to such compliments. Meanwhile her temperature shot up several degrees, especially when she took a good look at him. His slim-hipped, long-legged body was made to wear those crisp new jeans, and his shirt of unbleached muslin contrasted handsomely with his newly acquired tan.

Keeping her eyes down, Ellie grabbed her canvas purse from the kitchen counter. "Are you ready to go?" she asked.

"Anytime."

She scurried out the door ahead of him so that he couldn't get close enough to touch her. Even a courteous hand at her waist or elbow would have sent her senses into a tizzy. She needed a few moments to gather herself together and put things into perspective. This was an innocent evening out, a case of an employer showing his employee gratitude. This was *not* the senior prom.

She opened the passenger door of the blue rental car and scooted inside.

He sauntered after her, climbing behind the steering wheel with loose-limbed ease, bringing with him a subtle woodsy fragrance mingled with his own uniquely male scent. "What's wrong with you, Ellie?" he teased as he started the engine. "You remind me of one of those skittery ostriches."

"I'm just anxious," she answered quickly, having anticipated the question. She was behaving a bit strangely, after all. "It's been so long since I went out at night to a real restaurant, I don't know how to act. You might have to show me which fork to use and remind me not to slurp my soup."

"I'll signal you if you start to embarrass me with your atrocious table manners," he assured her dryly.

She relaxed some as the big luxury sedan glided along the mountain roads, smooth as a swan on water. She'd never ridden in such a fancy car, but she refrained from saying so. She was sure Zach already thought of her as a hick. Instead, she would at least try to be sophisticated. She wasn't completely ignorant of the ways of the world, she reminded herself. She did have a college degree.

She kept expecting Zach to ask her where he was supposed to take them, but he didn't. He drove an unwavering path through Ledbetter and around Lake Takanachi, asking casual questions about the sights, until he was in the parking lot of the Choctaw Inn. He must have studied a local map, she decided. Like most men, he probably didn't trust a woman to direct him anywhere.

"We're early," she said, checking the sturdy Timex watch she wore on her left wrist. "Do you want to walk by the lake before we go inside?" She had an ulterior motive. Once again she wanted to show him how tranquil life was around Rocky Ridge, and how further development would ruin everything.

He nodded his agreement, but his face had taken on a curious, guarded expression. Maybe he'd caught on to her game plan. With a shrug, Ellie led the way down a flight of stone steps that ended at a narrow, paved path.

She and Zach meandered down the shoreline among towering pine trees as the setting sun turned ripples on the water to fiery orange. Mockingbirds darted from tree to tree, chirping playfully at each other. A soft breeze brought with it the scent of evening. She couldn't have set the stage better herself.

Ellie picked up a rock and sliced it toward the water, watching with satisfaction as it skipped four times. "Mmm, I haven't been to the lake in a long time. It's always even prettier than I remember it. I wonder why SunnyLand, or some other developer, didn't try to capitalize on it before now?"

When Zach made no reply, she realized he'd halted on the path several feet behind her. He was staring out at the shimmering water, his thumbs shoved in his pockets, his expression intense.

She retraced her steps until she stood beside him. "Zach, what's wrong?"

He acted as if he didn't hear her. She was about to reach out and touch his sleeve when all at once a look of wonder fell over his face. "I remember this place. There's a fishing pier down at that end of the lake, isn't there?"

"There used to be, until they tore it down a few years ago," Ellie said as a small thrill stirred inside her breast.

Zach looked up at the Choctaw Inn on the hill above them. "And this place. Are there two wooden Indians standing by the door?"

She nodded eagerly, and the stirring intensified. His roots *were* here, dammit, right along with hers. Again she dared to hope for the impossible—that this red earth would reclaim its native son.

Seven

The peculiar sensation of déjà vu stayed with Zach throughout dinner. He haphazardly ordered the first item he saw on the menu, then hardly tasted the salad, prime rib and baked potato as images from the past flashed through his mind.

He remembered an old mobile home with a tattered awning that might well have been his home. There was a funny mongrel dog, too, with a shrill bark and a patch over one eye. And there was a man—not Zach's father—who gently held a small boy's hands around his first rod and reel.

Had that man been his uncle Clem?

"Is your steak too tough?" Ellie asked.

"Hmm? Oh, no, it's fine." As he carved off a bite of the succulent beef and popped it into his mouth, he realized he'd been neglecting his dining companion. This was to be his last dinner with Ellie. He ought to make the most of it. He firmly pushed all those old, useless memories to the back of his mind and concentrated on creating a special evening for her.

His gaze settled on the creamy skin revealed by the open neck of her dress. How could any red-blooded man ignore her when she was such a feast for the male senses? An intriguing bit of lace peeked out where her dress made a vee, and suddenly his hands itched to unfasten the next button, and then the next and the next, until she stood before him wearing only that lacy whatever-it-was.

An uncomfortable tightness settled in the region south of his belt. Jeez, he didn't need to concentrate on her *that* much. "How about dessert?" he asked abruptly. "I notice they have cherry cheesecake on the menu."

"Well ... I'm not finished with dinner yet."

"Or the double-fudge brownie. That one sounded good." Was dessert the only topic of conversation he could come up with? Rushing the woman through dinner wasn't exactly a suave move. The Bordeaux wine he'd ordered must have fogged his brain, although he recalled taking only a few sips.

"I'll decide in a while," she said mildly, and her gaze flickered over him like the blue tip of a flame.

Did she know what he was thinking? he wondered. He usually kept his feelings closely guarded, a necessity in the cold world of finance. But Ellie had a strange effect on him. His normally clear-minded common sense disappeared, as if it had dropped right out a hole in his brain.

He took another bite of his baked potato as he continued to watch her. She sipped her wine, closing her eyes to appreciate the taste as it swirled across her tongue. The purely sensual look on her face nearly undid him.

"Would you excuse me?" Without waiting for her consent, he left the table.

In the men's room he splashed water on his face. *Get a grip, Shaner!* He had found Ellie appealing, even desirable, almost from the first moment he'd known her. But no woman had ever gotten to him in such a sudden surge.

Judging from the way she sometimes looked at him through those sexy, half-closed eyes and ran the tip of her tongue across her full lower lip, her thoughts might well be headed in a similar direction. Certainly he hadn't imagined the spark between them that sometimes threatened to flare into a full-blown inferno. He allowed himself to savor the idea for a moment, then shook his head in frustration.

He could not, *would* not, take advantage of Ellie's small-town, country-girl innocence. She had made it clear that she wanted him to stay here, and frankly, the decision to sell to SunnyLand and get the hell out was becoming harder and harder to make. How much more difficult would his dilemma be if he and Ellie... How could he make love to the woman and then sell the ranch out from under her?

By the time he returned to the table, his resolve was firmly in place, his unruly thoughts corralled as securely as the ostriches back at the ranch.

"Did you decide on dessert?" he asked as he took his chair, returning his napkin to his lap with a flourish.

"I don't think I have room for sweets," she said, looking down at her almost-empty plate. "I'm afraid my appetite was anything but dainty tonight."

"Nonsense. I've never found a dainty appetite all that appealing. I'd rather a woman enjoy herself when I take her out to dinner."

She smiled. "That I have. Now, if you want dessert, you go ahead."

Zach shook his head. He was no more interested in eating now than he had been earlier. Maybe dancing would work off some of his excess... energy. After all, how romantic could a crowded, smoky, noisy kicker bar be? He signaled their waiter for the check.

* * *

The gravel parking lot of Hooper's was filled with Jeeps, pickup trucks and an occasional bad-ass hot rod. Zach's shiny rented Buick looked as out of place as a tuxedo at a tractor pull, and Zach himself felt the first stirrings of unease. Despite his boots and jeans, he was likely to stand out as obviously as his car.

Inside, the club was much as he had imagined—a cavernous, barnlike structure where the band played too loudly, the patrons drank too much and the men stared much too boldly at the women, particularly at Ellie. But there was a certain sense of fun here, too. No one seemed to take things too seriously, including who was partnered with whom on the crowded dance floor.

Zach and Ellie claimed one of the last free tables in the very back. A miniskirted waitress with a squat beehive of teased hair wasted no time bringing each of them a beer, carefully displaying her cleavage to Zach as she set the sweating cans on the table. She winked when he told her to keep the change.

"So, do you want to dance?" Ellie asked.

Zach eyed the dance floor with trepidation. Couples moved in well-orchestrated patterns, their booted feet sliding against sawdust on concrete to the rhythm of the music. "I don't know how to dance that way."

"Oh, that." She waved away his concern. "It's just a two-step. I can show you how in less than a minute."

His desire to hold Ellie in his arms for a legitimate purpose warred with his reluctance to look like a stumbling idiot. It hadn't occurred to him that he would be too ignorant about this form of dance to participate. "Ah, I think I'll watch for a while." He took a sip of his beer.

"Okay," she agreed, but her eloquent body language clearly stated that she wondered why he'd suggested coming here if he intended to sit in his chair all night.

It wasn't long before a young buck boldly approached her. "Well, howdy, Ellie. I haven't seen you out and about in a while."

"Been busy, Darryl. Oh, Darryl, I don't think you've met Zach Shaner, Clem's nephew. Zach, this is Darryl Granger. We went to high school together."

Zach stood, and the two men warily shook hands. Zach immediately disliked the man, with his wavy, sun-bleached hair and his too-tight jeans and his shiny gold rodeo-championship buckle.

Darryl sized Zach up at the same time, his eyes reflecting more curiosity than animosity, then returned his attention to Ellie. "How about a dance for old times' sake?"

"Sure, I'd love to—you don't mind, do you, Zach?"

Hell, yes, he minded! Just what "old times" were they thinking of? But what could he say and not sound like a jerk? He nodded and forced a smile. "Go ahead, have some fun."

She proceeded to do just that. Zach watched with ever-growing envy as the young cowboy swung Ellie around the floor during a spirited polka. They both laughed and clapped when it was over, and then another man, one old enough to be her father, claimed Ellie as a partner.

When she moved into the arms of a third man, Zach decided he'd had enough of Hooper's. If he'd wanted to spend the evening with a beer, he could have gone out by himself.

On the dance floor Ellie steeled herself as her energetic partner swung her off her feet and into another couple. She waved and nodded her apology, the best she could do since it was impossible to talk over the loud music. That's when she spotted Zach standing not fifteen feet away, an ominous expression on his face.

The song ended at an opportune moment. She thanked her partner, then wove her way through the sea of bodies until she reached Zach. "Did you change your mind?"

"No, I—"

The band started up again, cutting off the rest of his reply. The song was a slow one, and couples drifted into each other's arms to sway gently under the dimmed lights.

The temptation was one Ellie couldn't resist. She laid her hand on Zach's unyielding arm and leaned close to him so that he could hear her. "C'mon, Zach, anyone can do this dance."

There was just enough challenge in her words that she knew he couldn't say no. Then he was standing before her, his green eyes unreadable as he slid his arms around her waist and pulled her to him. She reciprocated by winding her arms around his neck and nestling her head against his shoulder.

Lord, he felt better than any man had a right to. His lean body was warm and firm against hers, and his hands roamed shamelessly over her back, causing her blood to pulse at a dangerous rate. His muslin shirt was enticingly rough against her cheek, and it smelled of soap and the great outdoors, just as the man did.

She recalled all too clearly what it had felt like when they'd kissed. Then, she'd thought the kiss a mistake, a subconscious reaction, a side effect from her excitement; she'd run from it like a skittish filly. But during dinner she'd decided her subconscious knew what it was doing. She wanted to feel that rock-hard mouth on hers again, so she could react to it like the woman she was.

She knew damn well that all her feminine wiles couldn't keep Zach on Rocky Ridge if he didn't want to stay. Only the land itself could draw him and hold him. But what she'd seen tonight had encouraged her—enough that she could risk more than she'd been willing to even hours earlier.

When the song ended, Zach made no move to release her. They stood together for countless eternal seconds, during which Ellie was afraid to move, afraid to breathe for fear of breaking the spell. Zach breathed enough for both of them. She could hear him hauling great gulps of air into his lungs.

At last she managed to tip her head back and look into his face. The expression she saw there was one of pure torture. "Zach?"

Slowly he loosened his hold on her. "I'd like to leave now," he said with deliberate calm.

"And go where?" Her voice came out throaty and seductive, though she hadn't consciously intended it that way.

"Home."

A thrill went through her whenever he referred to the Red Canyon as *home*. "And do what?"

"Don't push your luck, lady. I'm not in any mood to be teased." He turned and left the dance floor, giving her no opportunity to rebut.

Teased? she thought indignantly as she made her way to their table to retrieve her purse. She wouldn't think of playing games with Zach. Although he had been thoroughly polite and gentle with her, she sensed he could be a dangerous man if provoked.

No, teasing wasn't her aim. Her every look and gesture toward him came from her heart. Maybe it wasn't wise of her to be so open, but she'd never learned how to hide what she felt. Apparently Zach had. Her questions about his plans for the rest of the evening hadn't yielded a whole lot. She wasn't sure whether he was ticked off at her or he wanted to ravish her in the back seat.

He waited for her, stone faced, as she grabbed her bag. Then he swiftly led the way to the exit, giving Ellie no chance to say her good-nights to anyone.

"So what's the problem?" she asked when they were inside the car. "Are your boots giving you blisters?"

Zach shoved his key into the ignition and turned it hard, revving the motor. "I should think the problem would be obvious. I'm having a difficult time maintaining a proper employer-employee relationship with you."

"Same here." She took a deep breath, because she was about to head into deeper water. "Is there a law that says we have to?"

"Yeah, there is—Zach's Law."

"And that is . . . ?"

He pulled the car out of the parking lot, spitting gravel behind it. "Never indulge in a one-night stand with a woman who deserves better."

"I'm quite capable of deciding what I do and don't deserve," she retorted. "And anyway, does it have to be for only one night?" She held her breath waiting for his answer.

Minutes ticked by. Miles of moon-washed forest slipped by the car windows, and still Zach made no reply. Unexpectedly he turned off the main road, and Ellie realized he was heading for the scenic lookout she'd shown him on his last visit. He pulled off the dirt road and cut the engine.

Why here? Ellie wondered. She observed his strong profile, but his face revealed nothing. When he got out of the car and walked to the edge of the precipice, she followed, watching, waiting. Even the night creatures were oddly silent, as if they, too, waited. Only the muffled hiss of the nearby waterfall interfered with the absolute quiet.

"Dammit, Ellie," he finally said. Though his words weren't spoken loudly, they cracked the silence like a heavy spoon hitting an eggshell. "You have this crazy notion that I'm going to fall in love with this place, move down here and become a bird rancher. That isn't possible. I have a life in St. Louis, a house, a company to run, for God's sake." He grabbed her shoulders in a painfully tight grip and stared down at her with frightening intensity. "I'm not staying here, have you got that? I'm *not*."

"I think you fell in love with this place twenty-something years ago," she said, risking his further anger but unwilling to let the words go unspoken. "The mountains get in your blood, like a fever. And I think every hour you spend here, your temperature climbs a little higher. Your roots are here. You just won't admit it."

"No, *you* just won't face facts—" Abruptly he cut himself off, and with the swiftness of a striking snake he hauled her against him and covered her mouth with his. It was a harsh, bruising kiss, intended to intimidate.

It scared her, but it didn't make her want him any less. She sensed the confusion beneath his macho display, and again dared to hope that he would make the right decisions—right for him as well as her.

He broke the kiss, his breathing ragged, his face a mask of tortured desire. "If I spend the night in your bed, do you think it'll change my mind, Ellie? Because it won't. I have a fever, all right, but it has nothing to do with mountains or forests. I want you. But I won't make love to you if you think sex is going to tie me to you and the Red Canyon. It won't."

She stiffened with a fury of her own. "If you spend the night in my bed, it'll be because I want you, plain and simple. I don't bargain with my body."

He seemed to realize the insult he'd paid her, because his grip on her shoulders eased and his harsh expression softened. "I'm sorry, Ellie. I should know better than to think . . . Oh, hell. *Do* you want me?"

"Do you even have to ask?"

"And you understand—"

"I understand that you fully intend to abandon your legacy from your last surviving relative, and I still want you." Her words rang through the woods, sure and clear.

"And if I leave tomorrow, and you never see me again, you won't regret it?"

"No." The denial didn't come out as forcefully as she would have liked. Rather than think about tomorrow, she chose to concentrate on tonight. She ran her palm up the front of Zach's shirt, felt his heart beating inside his chest. Her fingertips connected with his neck, his beard-roughened jaw, then slowly moved around to the back of his head. His hair was soft. Before she knew it, the fingers of both hands were winnowing through the short, silky strands. She stood on tiptoe and pulled him to her.

There was nothing rough about this kiss. Hungry, yes; demanding, insistent and exciting, most definitely. But there was an underlying tenderness there, one of the qualities that had drawn her to Zach all along.

His tongue sought entrance to her mouth. She eagerly allowed it and wanted more—more contact between their bodies, more sensations. She wanted to drown herself in Zach, feel his strength all around her and inside her.

Ellie wasn't very experienced. She'd had a couple of relationships in college, both short-lived, through which she'd learned that infatuation wasn't the same as love. Although neither of those two young men had made the earth shake for her, she hadn't become jaded about sex. She'd always known that when the right man came along, it would be different.

And so far, it was. She had never felt such burning need—the need to give pleasure as well as receive. Zach spoke to both those needs when he unbuttoned the front of her dress and slid his hand beneath the denim to cup her breast. The smooth silk of her camisole rubbed against her sensitized nipple as he teased it with his thumb. She moaned, the needful sound echoing on the night air.

He meant to have her right here, she realized in some dim recess of her mind. But what he was doing felt so good. He had pushed her dress off her shoulders, letting the cool breeze caress her bare skin, and had dipped his head low to taste the valley between her breasts. She didn't want to spoil the flow of energy between them with her insignificant concerns. So few people lived down this road that chances were slim anyone would drive by.

She was about to offer to take off her dress so they could lie on it when the mood between them subtly changed. Zach's fevered kisses grew less so, his marauding hands stilled, his breathing slowed. Finally he issued a muffled curse and released her completely, turning his back. He put several feet of distance between them until he stood on the very edge of the precipice, looking out over the endless hills of the Kiamichis.

"Now what?" she cried, bereaved from the loss of his warmth, his nearness. Her control was so utterly shattered, her frustration so great, that for one second she had a wild urge to push him off the cliff.

"This isn't right," he murmured, still not facing her, "and all the rationalizing in the world won't make it right. I haven't been totally honest with you."

Ellie gulped the thin air. "You haven't?"

Zach shook his head. "Tomorrow your two weeks are up. I've decided to sell the Red Canyon to SunnyLand."

"*What?*"

Now he turned.

Feeling suddenly bare, she shoved her arms through the sleeves of her dress and clutched the front closed with one hand. "So that's what this is all about—the boots, the dinner, dancing.... You were trying to soften me up for the blow."

"I was trying to enjoy a nice evening with you because I knew it would be our last. I didn't expect this to happen." He gestured helplessly.

"What did you expect? And when were you planning to tell me about SunnyLand—when the bulldozers arrived?"

"I was going to tell you tomorrow, when the two weeks were officially up. But under the circumstances, you needed to know now."

"So I can go home and start working on my résumé? Scan the Help Wanted ads in the *Ostrich Gazette*?"

Zach sighed. "I thought this would change things . . . and I see it has," he said as she busily buttoned up her dress.

Oddly enough it didn't change things as much as he believed. She still wanted him. "I don't usually make love with men I'm furious with." She fastened every last button, right up to the neck.

"I wish you would at least try to understand my position. I can't continue to deplete my own finances with a venture that might never pay off. I have to do something, and there's no other alternative. The Forsythes were my first, last and only prospective buyers."

Ellie paid no attention as she started walking.

"Where are you going?" Zach demanded.

"Home. To pack. Looks like I'm out of a job."

"On foot? It must be three miles!"

"I need time to think."

Zach jumped in the car, started it, and drove up beside her with his window down. "Ellie, be reasonable. You can't walk home by yourself at night. Now get in the car."

"Leave me alone." With that she veered from the road, heading into the woods. She couldn't sit in the same car with him. She felt betrayed, stabbed in the back. All this time she'd thought he was gradually coming to see things her way, to understand the importance of the Red Canyon's ostrich operation to the community. But he understood nothing if he could blithely sell to that environmental nightmare of a developer.

She heard his car door open and then the sound of him blundering through the underbrush, chasing her. But in the dark he had no hope of catching her, not when she knew this countryside as well as the 'coons and 'possums and could creep with the stealth of an Indian. With small satisfaction she heard him curse again in defeat.

She hiked for about a quarter mile until she came back out on the main road. By that time her initial ire had faded a little. She began to wonder if Zach wasn't partly right. Not about SunnyLand—never. But maybe she had been hoping to tie him to her with lovemaking. Or with love, period. No matter how many times he said he wouldn't live here, a part of her still hoped.

Was she falling in love with Zach Shaner? If that was the case, she was the one most likely to feel ties between them. She would be the one reaching for empty space and crying in the dark, while he would return to St. Louis unscathed. What a dope she was. She'd lost her ranch, and possibly her heart, as well.

Zach poured himself a cup of coffee the next morning, banging the pot down with unnecessary force. He'd stayed up last night for an hour after he'd arrived home, waiting for Ellie. Waiting in the dark, because he hadn't wanted to give her the satisfaction of knowing he worried about her. As soon as he saw her slender form trooping up the driveway, he'd gone to bed, where he'd lain awake even longer, regretting the loss of what might have been.

He had to sell to SunnyLand. He didn't have another choice, did he?

Ellie entered the kitchen, looking unusually rumpled and grumpy to boot. Irrationally Zach wanted to kiss away those furrows between her eyebrows. "You know, there's a job waiting for you at the ranch SunnyLand is selling all the birds to. That's part of the deal."

She gave him a look that said "drop dead" as she headed out the kitchen door, coffee cup in hand.

"Where are you going?"

She paused, leaning against the doorframe. "Not that it matters at this point, but I'm going to check and see if those hormone-deficient ostriches have laid any eggs." She slammed the door behind her.

Let there be an egg, he prayed. If there was just one, he would delay accepting SunnyLand's offer. He would give Ellie another week or two and see if she could really sell an egg for a thousand dollars.

He waited fifteen minutes. And when he heard nothing from Ellie, he headed into the office to make his call to Phyllis Quincy. Since it was Sunday, he called her home number.

"Oh, hello, Mr. Shaner," she said with surprising coolness. He soon discovered why. After he stated the purpose of his call, there was a long pause and a lot of throat clearing. "Well, Zach, we have a slight hitch. There's some litigation pending in Arkansas regarding one of our other parks. Nothing major—it'll all be worked out soon enough."

Nothing major? Just a poisoned stream and several broken promises. Guilt burned in his gut. He'd conveniently forgotten about those lawsuits Ellie had told him about.

"But the problem," she continued, "is that SunnyLand has been slapped with a...a ridiculous court injunction. We can't acquire any more land for the Choctaw Park until this matter is cleared up. So I'm afraid our offer is null and void."

Zach shot out of his chair in pure shock. This couldn't be happening to him.

"Of course, we'll be happy to resume negotiations when the injunction's been lifted."

"And when do you anticipate that?"

"Oh, two months, perhaps three at the most. We'll be in touch."

After she hung up, Zach nearly strangled himself with the phone cord. Three months! What was he supposed to do until then? One thing was for sure. He would have to do some serious backpedaling with Ellie. He had practically fired her.

The kitchen door slammed again, signaling her return. Zach emerged from the office, bracing himself to eat a hearty portion of crow.

Ellie took one look at him, and her scowl dropped away to be replaced by honest concern. "Zach? Are you okay? You look like you stuck your face in a sack of flour."

He made his way to the kitchen table and sat down, trying not to let his shakiness show. "So, Ellie, how would you like to stay on here awhile?"

She narrowed her eyes suspiciously. "What do you mean?"

He could have lied to her and said he'd changed his mind, earning her unceasing good will, but that would only cause more trouble down the line when she found out the real story. "I mean SunnyLand withdrew its offer. Temporarily, that is. So it looks like the Red Canyon will have to go on as is for a while, and I would be ever so grateful if you would stay on as the manager."

A slow smile spread across her face. "Well, well, this is an interesting situation," she said as she strutted around the kitchen. "Ol' Phyllis reneged on her offer?"

"It has to do with the litigation in Arkansas you told me about," he said. "It should be cleared up in two or three months. But meanwhile..." He shrugged helplessly.

"Meanwhile, someone has to run the place. Hmm," she said, tapping her chin with her forefinger. "Some of those jobs advertised in the *Ostrich Gazette* sound pretty good."

"You wouldn't!"

"You fired me," she retorted.

"Not in so many words. Anyway, I'm hiring you back. I'll double your salary."

"Double nothing. That's a pretty safe offer."

"That was a feeble attempt at a joke. I know money wouldn't keep you here if you really wanted to leave. But you don't want to leave," he said with certainty. "So what do you want, Ellie? Do you want me to grovel?"

She pretended to consider this. "That has a certain appeal, but no, there's only one thing that will keep me here—one little condition."

"And that is?" He dreaded her next words.

"You stay here and work with me."

Eight

Damn, it was hot. The back of Zach's neck prickled from the heat as he stood in front of the kitchen sink doing the breakfast dishes. A small, clattery, window air-conditioning unit failed to keep up with the upward-galloping temperature of an early, unseasonable heat wave. Or maybe it was his latest run-in with Ellie that made his blood so hot.

At first he hadn't taken Ellie's preposterous demand seriously. But he'd soon found out just how tough willed a blue-eyed wisp of a girl could be when she wanted something badly enough. She had turned a deaf ear to logic and reason. She had stood unflinchingly as he'd ranted and raved and accused her of blackmail. Even his coldest, most intimidating *look*, which had reduced many a hard businessman to stuttering, hadn't affected her. Either he had to stay at the ranch and work, or she was packing up and leaving.

His business partner, Jeff Hodges, had laughed himself into a case of hiccups when Zach had explained his dilemma over the phone. He'd been hoping that Jeff would come up with some overriding reason why Zach couldn't take a few weeks off to look after his inheritance. But Jeff, the traitor, had blithely assured Zach that the world of finance would function just fine without him, then reminded him that he hadn't taken a vacation in three years. "Hell, maybe this little enforced holiday will keep you from getting that ulcer you've been pushing for," he'd said.

So Zach was stuck with life at the Red Canyon. And ever since Ellie had issued her ridiculous ultimatum, and he had tersely agreed to stay, they'd hardly uttered a word to each another.

For two full days Zach had done nothing but growl and glare while Ellie remained maddeningly unaffected. At least she wasn't smug. She had forced him into this untenable situation not out of malice, but to comply with her own slightly twisted agenda for his life. That was the only thing that saved her from a really ruthless act on his part—like turning the birds loose into the woods, torching the ranch and forgetting he'd ever heard of it.

Now he scrubbed the dishes with a vengeance, deliberately splatting every bubble in the sink with his sponge. What this place needed was an electric dishwasher! And a modern refrigerator and a microwave and a stove that didn't smoke and scorch their food and heat up the kitchen like a blast furnace. At the first opportunity he was driving to the nearest appliance store, and to hell with any notions Ellie had about saving money. He'd put it all on a credit card if he had to.

And while he was out, he would buy some lumber and paint and the tools he needed to fix up this shack. He might be stuck with this place for another two or three months, but there was no law that said he had to be uncomfortable while he stayed here.

He wondered how much it would cost to put in an extra bathroom, not to mention central air.

"Zach! Zach, come quick!"

The hysterical shriek broke through his disgruntled reverie. Ellie! Oh, God, what was wrong? With visions of blood and broken bones and fire and mayhem, he dropped a cup into the dishwater with a plop and dashed for the door.

Ellie, mercifully in one piece, met him as he burst from the house. She grabbed his arm and dragged him toward the barn. "Come quick, come quick," she repeated breathlessly.

"Ellie, what's wrong?"

He soon found out there was nothing wrong. For a change, something was right. With a silencing finger to her lips, Ellie slowed and urged Zach to follow her quietly to the first ostrich pen. "Look there," she whispered.

In the middle of the pen, sitting in the sand, was a huge white egg.

Ellie was smiling as if she'd just won the lottery. "Isn't it great? Isn't it fantastic? No, it's even better than that. It's a miracle. Finally, *finally!*"

Zach tried to remain aloof. After all, this madly grinning woman standing beside him was the same one who had blackmailed him. But her contagious enthusiasm sneaked up on him, until he found himself grinning right along with her. "Congratulations," he said. "Does this make us grandparents, or what?"

She gave a disgusted snort. "I don't claim any kinship to those stupid birds. The idiot hen laid her egg right there on the ground, when there's a perfectly good nest inside the shelter. How do we get it out of there?"

"I was just going to ask you the same question. We can't leave a fragile egg in there for long. One of our fine feathered friends is liable to step on it or peck a hole in the shell."

"You're right. But just try to go in there and pick it up."

Challenged, Zach replied, "Okay, I will. Where's an empty feed bag?"

Ellie fetched one from the barn. But the moment Zach unfastened the gate, visions of heroism in his head, eight feet of incensed ostrich charged toward him, its feathers puffed out in a threatening display.

All right, Zach thought as he backed away, so he was no St. George. But that beast was *worse* than a dragon. Still, there had to be a way to prevent the bird from slicing and dicing him.

"I've got an idea," Ellie whispered, as if the bird could overhear. "You stay here and distract him. I'll come in from the other gate inside the barn, sneak through the shelter, grab the egg and be gone before he knows what's happened."

Zach nodded. "All right, but you be careful. If that rooster even looks your way, run like hell."

"Don't worry, I will. I want that egg, but I'm not willing to make a trip to the hospital to get it."

Zach did his best imitation of a matador, standing just inside the open gate with his feed sack, waving it in the agitated bird's face every time it got close enough to strike. The strategy worked. From the corner of his eye he saw Ellie zip in from the shelter, grab the egg and vanish.

"Okay, I'm clear," she called. Zach immediately slipped out the gate and latched it firmly, then took a deep breath to steady himself. The ostrich looked around, startled. Then one of the hens caught his attention, and he began courting her. He never seemed to notice that his potential offspring had been stolen. As Ellie had told Zach more than once, ostriches weren't known for their intelligence.

"I got it, I got it," Ellie cried as she came out of the barn, cradling the egg to her body as if it were a newborn baby. And it was, Zach supposed.

He came up to her and touched the hard shell with his fingertip. The egg was as big as a saucer, and the shell was warm from the sun and slightly rough.

"That's truly amazing," he said. Even more amazing was the radiant look on Ellie's face. She glowed with the happiness of triumph. Unable to resist, he leaned down and captured her mouth with his, knowing that since her arms were full there was nothing she could do to stop him.

She didn't even try. Rather, she accepted his kiss with sweetness and warmth and provokingly responsive lips. Instead of the quick, triumphant kiss he'd planned, he found himself with his arms around Ellie, dragging the elastic band from her hair so he could bury his hands in the smooth silk, devouring all the nourishing enthusiasm that had somehow gotten channeled into the sensual dance of mouth against mouth, tongue against tongue.

Over the past two days he had managed to squelch his formidable craving for Ellie's body by holding on to his anger. Every time he felt that telltale stirring of lust in the pit of his stomach, he would remind himself how furious he was with her, how unreasonable she was, and he would keep the gnawing desire at bay. But always it lingered in the background, waiting for the right moment.

Funny, he couldn't summon even a pinch of anger toward her right now.

"Mmm, Zach?" she managed.

"Mmm, what?" he murmured.

"Unless you want a quart of raw egg down the front of your shirt, you might want to back up a bit."

Oh, the egg. He was lucky he hadn't unnerved her so thoroughly that she'd dropped the damn thing. Reluctantly he loosened his hold on her and stepped back, searching the depths of her eyes for a reaction. The potent kiss had left him dizzy. Or maybe it was simply Ellie that made him dizzy, holding on to that egg with maternal pride.

Her eyes were maddeningly secretive, and she continued to smile. "Does this mean you're not mad at me any more?" she asked.

He hadn't expected such a calm reaction from her. "Oh, I'm still mad," he assured her, positive that he would regain his irritation once his desire receded. "But this occasion called for a kiss, regardless."

Weak rationalization, Shaner. It was the way she held that egg that had made him kiss her, that made him want to do it again. His imagination was playing tricks on him. Instead of an egg, he saw her holding a baby. *His* baby. "Now if that isn't the dumbest—"

"What's dumb?" she asked indignantly.

He hadn't realized he'd spoken aloud. "Uh, nothing. Shouldn't we get that thing into an incubator or something?"

"We have nine days before we have to incubate it. I think we should take it to town and show everybody. Ben Potee will be beside himself. He owns the first egg."

"I hope he's not fond of omelets," Zach said, gradually recovering.

"And this is only the beginning," she crowed. "I'll be tomorrow we have another egg, and the next day another. And when we have a half dozen or so, I'll drive down to Texas and sell 'em to Duane Scoggins."

"Better yet, we could fly down," Zach suggested. "That way we could make the trip in one day."

"And then we'll have five or six thousand dollars. Imagine."

"Five or six thousand dollars that belongs to the share holders," he reminded her.

"Not all of it. Every third egg is ours, remember? And anyway, I'm going to convince the shareholders to reinvest their profits. Now that I have something to show them, it'll be a cinch to sell shares." And she was off, spinning her dreams of a rosy future for the Red Canyon. For once, Zach was inclined to dream a little, too.

Ellie hummed as she used pillows and wadded-up towels to make a cozy nest for the egg in a covered picnic basket. She'd finished feeding and watering the birds in record time, offering the fruitful trio an extra treat of lettuce, which had been greedily devoured. She'd barely escaped with her fingers intact.

Now she and Zach were planning to celebrate with lunch at Rosie's Café.

She hadn't felt this happy in months, not since before Clem had died. Her overgrown hens were producing—one of them, anyway; SunnyLand had been put on hold; and Zach . . . Zach had kissed her again. After the stunt she'd pulled, forcing him to remain here, she thought for sure he'd lost any hope of more than a business relationship with him.

She'd *had* to do it, she told herself for the umpteenth time. Keeping Zach's feet firmly planted on Rocky Ridge soil was more important than any personal aspirations she had, whatever those might be. She just knew that if he stayed here long enough, he wouldn't be able to leave.

Now it appeared Zach might not be lost to her after all. She sighed as she closed the lid on the basket. Yes, she was falling in love with the man, not the smartest thing she'd ever done. She vowed to keep her priorities straight. First she had to get him to commit himself to the land and the ranch. Then she'd work on a commitment to her.

"Ellie, girl, you're putting the train ahead of the engine," she murmured as she left her bedroom. Zach might

be keen on taking her to bed, but that was a heckuva lon
way from love and marriage. She wasn't altogether sure h
even *liked* her.

"It's about time," said Zach, who was waiting impa
tiently for her. "I'm starving. What were you doing, pu
ting a diaper on that thing?" He nodded toward the baske

"Everything but. I had to put an identifying sticker on i
It's important to keep one egg straight from another, so w
can know for sure who the parents are for each hatchling.

Zach peeked in at the egg, nestled in its swaddling. "Ir
teresting. But we don't know the parentage. That is, w
know Big John is the father, but which hen actually laid th
egg, Maizy or Daisy?"

Ellie shrugged. "Those two hens are sisters, so it doesn
much matter. And you shouldn't name livestock. It's a ba
idea to get sentimentally attached."

He seemed offended at the idea that he might be gettin
attached to the ugly birds. "The names are for clarity only
not sentimentality. C'mon, let's go."

They drove into town, as eager to show off the egg a
proud parents would be of a firstborn child. They stoppe
first at Rosie's Café. With a flourish, Ellie set the basket o
their table.

"Hi, Marjean," she greeted the elderly waitress. Then sh
whispered, "You want to have a look inside my basket?"

The woman's faded blue eyes sparkled as she lifted the li
Then she squealed in delight. "You got an egg! My lan
look at the size of that sucker. Betty! Rita! Come here an
see this. You won't believe it!"

Before long there was a crowd at their table, each perso
vying to get a peek at the gigantic egg. The questions cam
thick and fast. How much did it weigh? When would th
hens lay more? When would Ellie be ready to sell chicks, s
other folks could get in on this marvelous business? Coul
she really sell that egg for a thousand dollars?

She could, she assured them. Just that morning she'd talked to the rancher in Texas, and he was ready and willing to pay a thousand apiece. He knew the Red Canyon's birds were from good stock. He'd helped Ellie and Clem choose many of the birds, some of them from his own flock.

Then came the most satisfying question of all. "Can I buy some egg shares?"

Ellie looked at Zach, silently pleading with him to let her resume bartering.

He returned her gaze, first with exasperation, then finally with resignation. Slowly he nodded. "Yeah, sure, why not?"

They got more IOUs than cash, and one woman tried to give them a goat. But Ellie didn't mind. The trading floor was open again, and business was flourishing. Zach's presence, she noticed, seemed to lend credibility to her transactions.

After they had paraded up and down the boardwalks, entering every shop and milking the publicity of the first ostrich egg for all it was worth, Ellie suggested they head for Ben Poteet's place. It was his egg, after all. He ought to get a look at it.

Zach agreed and soon they were on the narrow road that passed the scenic lookout. Ellie couldn't help but remember what happened the last time they'd traveled this way. She kept her gaze glued to the road ahead of her as they passed the scene of that wanton embrace, but she felt a curling of heat deep inside her as her thoughts ran rampant. Fortunately Zach's attention was on his driving, so he couldn't notice the color she was sure flooded her face. If he remembered anything about last Saturday night, he gave no indication.

Ellie made him stop every time she saw people on their front porches or working in their yards. Then she would hop out of the car and show off the contents of the basket as admirers oohed and ahhed. Crusty old Ben was no exception. He actually smiled when he saw the evidence of Ellie's diligence and patience.

"You know, Ellie, I was beginning to think you were full of baloney," he said in his forthright way. "But I'll be darned if those ugly birds can't lay eggs. When do I get my money?"

"Well, it would be more cost-effective for me to sell a big batch of eggs at one time," she said. "So I'll probably wait till the end of the week. But . . . gee, Ben, I was kinda hoping you would reinvest."

"Reinvest? The whole thousand dollars? Aw, now, Ellie, I need that money."

"Okay, not the whole thousand. Just the profit."

"Five hundred?" He pulled off his tractor cap and scratched his head through his thick white hair. "Mebbe. I'll think on it."

Back on the road, Zach laughed out loud. "You know, Ellie, if you ever want a job in St. Louis, I'll give you one. I never saw anyone sweet-talk money out of people the way you do."

"I'm highly motivated." She opened the window and waved to a boy on a skinny horse. "There's just one more stop I want to make before we go home. You don't mind, do you?"

"It's your show. Where to?"

"Head toward the airstrip. I hope this car has good suspension."

Zach understood what she meant when she instructed him to turn onto a narrow, rutted, red-dirt road that climbed up the mountain at a forty-five-degree angle. The rental car bounced and jiggled and bottomed out several times as Zach did his best to negotiate around the car-eating potholes.

"Who are we going to see?" he asked just as a house came into view, a little gray frame cabin that looked as if it was about to fall down. In the distance was another building in similar condition, surrounded by several large pens filled with chickens. Another pen housed . . . a cow? No, it was the biggest hog Zach had ever seen.

"My family lives here," Ellie answered, straightening her spine and throwing back her shoulders. "This is where I grew up." She was almost daring him to make some comment.

Was she afraid he wouldn't approve? Hell, if this was where she'd grown up, and she'd gone to college and was making something of herself, that was a point in her favor.

In all honesty, though, he had to admit that if he hadn't gradually been indoctrinated into the Rocky Ridge culture, this place would have thrown him for a loop. Now he simply saw it as evidence of an incredible will to survive and be independent.

As he shut off the car, two huge shepherd-mix dogs came barreling around the corner of the house, barking and snarling like hounds from hell.

"Don't worry, they're harmless," Ellie said as she nonchalantly got out of the car. The moment they saw her, the dogs hunkered down in submissive postures, tails wagging, whining hopefully. She petted them both and crooned to them. When she was finished, they ran to Zach and repeated the performance. Zach gave them each a cautious pat. He thought again of that mongrel dog with a patch over its eye. Had that been his dog? What had become of it? His parents hadn't allowed him to have a dog when he was growing up in St. Louis.

As he and Ellie climbed a set of precariously leaning steps to the wide front porch, the door opened and a stout, gray-haired woman bustled through it. "Ellie! Ellie, land sakes, we haven't seen you in forever." With that she enveloped Ellie in a hearty hug.

Ellie bore it with moderate patience, holding the basket at arm's distance and with an iron grip. She looked at Zach. "It's been all of a week and a half," she said in an aside, which the older woman didn't seem to hear.

"And who's this with you?"

"Mama, this is Zach Shaner, Clem's nephew."

"Jerry and Frannie's boy?" Her smile faded as she scrutinized Zach with a critical eye. Then she reached up and grabbed his chin, turning his face from side to side as Ellie looked on, trying not to laugh.

"You've got more of Clem in you than either of your folks, I think," she declared, apparently satisfied.

Ellie threw him an I-told-you-so look.

"Zach, you can call me Aunt Flo," the older woman said as they went inside. "Everybody does."

In the cramped living room, Zach was introduced to Ellie's father, Ron, who grudgingly allowed Ellie to kiss him on the cheek, then acknowledged Zach with a nod before returning his attention to a hunting magazine. Both of the Kessler parents were older than Zach would have expected. Or maybe this harsh life just made them appear so.

The main room of the house was, like the Red Canyon's, crowded with furniture that had once been nice quality, but which was now worn, sagging and much repaired. There was a feeling of "making do," with everything patched, right down to the older man's slippers. Something was odd about the room, and Zach finally figured out what it was. There were no light fixtures or electric lamps. Just a single kerosene lamp.

"Why don't we go to the kitchen and see what goodies you brought in the basket?" Flo suggested to Ellie.

"Oh, the basket!" Ellie exclaimed, as if she'd forgotten about it. "It's not goodies, exactly, and I want Papa to see, too. And Jimmy. Where is he?"

"Playing baseball, like he does every day of the week," Flo said, clicking her tongue. "Can't get him to do a lick of work around here since he got accepted to college."

"Jimmy's going to U of Arkansas on a baseball scholarship," Ellie explained to Zach.

"Never mind about Jimmy," Flo said impatiently. "You've got my curiosity up. Come on, now, open that basket."

Ellie complied, allowing her mother to peer inside.

"Son of a gun," Flo murmured. That got Ron out of his chair to have a look. As if by magic, his whole mood changed. Before Zach's eyes the older man became animated, smiling even. "This is the first one, you say?" he asked Ellie.

"Laid just this morning."

"Maybe the weather turning so warm had something to do with it," he said thoughtfully. "Now, which egg is ours?"

"Number four. In a couple of weeks you'll have a thousand dollars," she said confidently. "Isn't that about what you need to get electricity brought in?"

"Electricity?" Ron repeated. "Hogwash. We been gettin' along without wires and sparks for more than a half century. Don't see no reason to change now."

"But, Papa," Ellie said, "wouldn't it be nice to have an electric washing machine?" Out of Ron's view, Flo nodded vigorously.

"No," he said flatly. "Ellie, honey, I don't think you should sell our egg. I want you to hatch it. And when the chick is big enough, you can bring it here and we'll put it in with the chickens."

Ellie's face brightened. "That's a wonderful idea. You'll get a lot more from your investment that way. I can sell a chick for anywhere from—"

"No, no, no!" Ron broke in. "We want to keep the bird
And when we butcher the next hog, I want to buy another
egg and hatch it. Then we'll have a pair, and we can start
breeding our own. Isn't that the idea?"

Ellie beamed. "That's right, Papa. Oh, but you know,
ostrich eggs don't hatch as easy as chicken eggs. And sometimes the chicks die. Are you willing to take that risk?"

"Ellie, you've been raising birds since before you could
walk. If anyone can hatch a healthy chick, you can."

As they continued to make plans for the birds, something clicked in Zach's mind. Even Flo's incredible cherry
pie didn't distract him from his new revelation. He began
mentally replacing the antiquated kitchen appliances with
new ones—an electric stove, a refrigerator and a sink with
running water instead of a pump. He saw ostrich eggs
translated into some simple comforts for two decent people. And he wondered how he could have been so selfish,
just that morning, when he'd cursed the Red Canyon's lack
of a dishwasher.

So, this was what Ellie's plan was all about. Getting the
locals interested in ostriches wasn't just a matter of keeping
the developers out of Rocky Ridge. She meant to restore
pride to its people, her parents included.

"So, what did you think?" Ellie asked as they drove back
down the mountain. His mood was unreadable. Was he
shocked? Disgusted? During the entire visit with her family, he had kept his forceful personality in the background,
treating them with quiet respect. He had even praised her
mother's pie. But all the while, his sharp eyes had taken in
every detail.

"I think your parents are nice people. And I hope their
chick hatches healthy and stays that way."

"Is that all?"

"What do you want me to say? That I'm appalled at the way your family lives, at how you grew up? I was a little shocked, I guess. That's what you intended, isn't it?"

Suddenly she was ashamed of herself. "You're right, I wanted to shock you. You must be getting pretty tired of me manipulating you, trying to get you to see things my way."

Unexpectedly he grinned at her. "But you're so good at what you do," he said. Then the smile faded. "Um, Ellie, I've been thinking. I ought to return this rental car—it's costing a fortune, not to mention what I'm spending for hangar space for my plane at the Muskogee airport."

She tamped down the panic that rose in her chest. She should have known it would happen sooner or later. He was calling her bluff. He had probably figured out by now that she would never willingly abandon her duties at the Red Canyon.

He was leaving.

Guilt nagged at her heart, pricking her with needle-sharp arrows. She never should have tried to keep him here against his will. "I guess that would make sense." To her horror, tears filled her eyes. She kept her head turned sharply away from Zach, staring out the passenger window. But first one telltale sniffle, then another, alerted him to her wretched state.

He stopped the car in the middle of the road. "Ellie, look at me." When she didn't obey, he reached over and cupped her wet cheek in his hand, gently turning her head until she faced him. "What the hell's wrong with you?"

She tried to come up with a suitable lie and couldn't. "I don't want you to leave," she admitted.

"It'll only be for a couple of days," he said with a confused frown.

It took a few moments, but slowly his words penetrated her brain. "You're . . . you're coming back?"

"Oh, that's rich. Do I have any choice?"

She took a steadying breath. "Yes, actually, you do. You can stay in St. Louis if you want, Zach. I'll stay here and take care of the birds for as long as you need me to. I was wrong to keep you here against your wishes."

He stared at her, studying her, perhaps trying to guess what new game she was playing.

"I'm on the level this time, Zach. You do what you have to."

Suddenly his face broke into a ridiculous smile. "Why, I wouldn't *dream* of staying in St. Louis. Things are just getting interesting." He trailed one finger down her cheek, her chin, her throat, all the way down to the gentle swell of her breast.

Her nipple hardened in swift response. She abandoned all her practical plans as Zach's touch lit her body on fire.

He leaned closer. Her willpower was minimal. She closed her eyes, anticipating another of his soul-searing kisses, when a loud, impatient honk jolted her.

Zach jumped, too. There was a truck full of lettuce behind them. He put the car in gear and floored it, his face a picture of irritation and regret.

Yeah, things were getting *interesting,* all right.

Nine

———

Ellie sat cross-legged on the braided rug in the cabin's main room and surveyed the growing nursery with a lump in her throat. Three eggs, each in its own basket. Three eggs in four days. It was really happening, just like she and Clem had pictured it through all those months and years of work.

"Oh, Clem," she said on a sigh. "I wish you were here to see this." And she wished someone else were here, too. Zach had been gone four days, and she was half-afraid he wasn't coming back. Maybe when he'd arrived in St. Louis, he'd changed his mind about spending time on the ranch. Then again, he'd given his word that he would return. She had to believe he would keep that promise.

She waited for the phone to ring. Surely Zach would be calling her any minute now, telling her when to pick him up at the airstrip. There was work to be done in the garden, but she refused to leave the phone. What if she missed his call?

A noise at the kitchen door made her jump to her feet, senses alert. "Who's there?" she called out, grabbing the first likely weapon, a heavy Bible from the bookshelf.

"Whom were you expecting?" a familiar voice called back.

Relief washed over her as Zach came around the corner. She put down the Bible, then had to restrain herself from rushing into his arms like a lovesick puppy. "Where'd you come from? How'd you get here from the airport?"

"I came from St. Louis, and I didn't arrive at the airport. I drove. The things I needed to bring wouldn't fit on the plane."

She couldn't stand not touching him. *The land and the ranch first, then me,* she silently chanted as she took his big, strong hand in hers and gave it a welcoming squeeze. "I'm glad you're back. Collecting eggs by myself is no fun."

His eyes lit up, and a crooked grin caught one corner of his mouth. "Eggs? There are more?"

"See for yourself." She pointed to the line of baskets.

"Well, I'll be damned," he said as he walked over to stare at the eggs, then leaned down to touch each one of them. When his examination was complete, he straightened and turned on her, his face stern. "Ellie, you didn't collect the other two by yourself, did you?"

His concern touched her. "Lucky for me, they were both laid in the nests. They were easy to collect. One came from Maizy or Daisy, the other from the duo."

"Napoleon and Josephine," he corrected her. "None yet from Larry, Curly, and Moe?"

"Maybe if you wouldn't give them such horrible names, they would cooperate. Honestly!"

He obviously enjoyed her exasperation. "Is that the only reason you're glad to see me? To help you collect eggs?"

The deep timbre of his voice and the fire in his eyes reached right to the pit of her stomach . . . and lower. There seemed to be a new purpose to his teasing, as if he had a definite agenda on his mind. In fact, she felt she had only to step closer, her face upturned, and he would . . .

No. She'd done a lot of thinking during the past four days. And the conclusion she'd reached was that no matter how tempting it was to give in to the attraction between them, she couldn't until the Red Canyon's future was firmly settled. She had no idea how long he planned to stay. She couldn't stop him from walking away, but she did know that the closer she let herself get to him, the harder it would be when he left.

"There are other reasons I'm glad to see you," she said, tilting her head provocatively. "The garden needs weeding. And I'm sick to death of my own cooking. Now, what all did you bring that was so dang big it wouldn't fit on your plane?"

She saw a flicker of disappointment cross his features before his smile returned. "Come see for yourself."

Her next surprise was his car. She gave a low whistle as she examined the silver Jaguar from fender to fender. "Wait till the folks around here get a load of this machine. Lord, what *did* you bring?" Behind the fancy car was a U-Haul trailer—a big one.

Zach ceremoniously opened the trailer doors for her, then stood back with his arms crossed, waiting for her reaction.

"Oh, *Zach.* A washing machine! And an electric range, a microwave oven and . . . is that a dishwasher?"

"Uh-huh."

"Did you move these from your house?"

He laughed. "No, I bought them just for the Red Canyon. One of my clients is in the appliance business. These are older models, dented, last year's colors. He was so grateful I kept him out of bankruptcy court, he practically gave them to me."

"They don't look old and dented to me." There were
other things in the trailer, as well, most notably a bunch of
power tools, some lumber and paint. Zach's intentions were
obvious, and her hopes soared. "Why, you're going to turn
this place into a palace!"

"A *palace* might be overstating my capabilities, but I am
going to make some sorely needed improvements." His next
words sent her hopes plummeting. "If I'm going to find a
buyer, I need to make things look a little more inviting."

She bit her tongue to keep from arguing. That was another decision she'd made recently. She wasn't going to tell
Zach what to do with the Red Canyon. She had shown him
Rocky Ridge, with all its wonders and its shortcomings. She
was confident he understood her goals when it came to the
ostrich operation. She had figured out that she couldn't
make him want to stay. Now she would have to count on the
mountains to work their magic on him.

Meanwhile she would do her best to stay out of his decisions. She never wanted to be haunted by the possibility that
she'd somehow tricked him, manipulated him or wooed him
into throwing his lot in with hers.

Maybe it wasn't a palace, but the Red Canyon was certainly looking spiffy these days, Ellie thought as she went
about her chores. Zach was a genius once he got his hands
on a few power tools. Working every weekend over the past
couple of months, and sometimes for a few days during the
week, he had completely rebuilt front and back porches on
both halves of the cabin, replaced pieces of the wood sid-
ing, patched the roof, updated the electrical wiring and
painted everything in sight. He'd also installed the modern
appliances in the kitchen, along with new oak cabinetry and
a pretty navy blue vinyl floor.

The washing machine sat on the back porch because there
wasn't room anyplace else, but Zach planned to enclose a

portion of the porch to make a utility room. The cabin was starting to look like a two-page spread from a glossy home-and-garden magazine.

"Nesting," Ellie called it. In her more fanciful moments, she imagined Zach was the rooster, preparing a cozy nest for his hen. Zach, of course, hotly denied that he planned to remain here any longer than it took to sell the place. He was merely making the Red Canyon a more attractive investment, he maintained.

He had, in fact, shown the property to two more would-be ostrich ranchers. Had Ellie only imagined the look of relief that had crossed Zach's face when each potential buyer had ended up deciding against the purchase? Maybe that had merely been wishful thinking on her part.

She paused a moment to watch Zach as he worked on his latest project, repairing and refinishing an old pedestal table he had found in the barn. She remembered what he'd told her about wanting to be a carpenter earlier in his life. It was sad that he hadn't pursued that career, she thought, because he didn't merely enjoy working with wood. The work actually transformed him. As he toiled in the hot June sun, sanding the oak surface of the table with a palm sander, then pausing to run his hands over the smooth surface, his face glowed with a warm satisfaction she'd never seen there before. She imagined him running his hands over her body with that same look on his face and shivered despite the heat.

"That looks mighty fine," she called to him, staying a safe distance from his tanned, sweat-slicked body. His jeans, once so crisp and new, had grown soft and faded from work and the wash, molding to his muscular thighs and hips. His hair now sported those golden sun streaks she'd only dreamed about when they'd first met, and it was longer, too. He was not the same rigid, uptight businessman she'd met back in April, and she couldn't help but believe it was this land, this ranch, that had made the change.

"This is a fine piece of furniture," he agreed. "When I get it finished, let's put it in the kitchen in place of that boxy monstrosity we eat on now."

"A smaller table would be nice. It's getting a mite crowded in that kitchen with all the new toys. Listen, I'm going down to the barn to check on the eggs."

"For at least the tenth time today," he said teasingly.

"I can't help myself—it's day forty-two, remember?"

He grinned. "You won't let me forget. I'll walk down there with you. I could use a break anyway, and there's something I want to talk to you about." He pulled a bandanna out of his back pocket and wiped his face like any good farmer. Yep, he was starting to belong here, Ellie thought, suppressing her amusement. He grabbed his T-shirt from where he'd hung it on a forsythia bush, and they started for the barn.

Ellie shoved her hands in her pockets as they walked side by side. How she'd managed to keep her hands off Zach during all these weeks, she would never know. Sometimes she itched to touch him, to bury her fingers in that thick, soft hair, to wrap herself around him and taste again of his mouth, so rich, so full of...Zach. Even now, engaged in the most innocent activity, she could smell the heat and sunshine and hard work emanating from his body, and it was all she could do to control herself.

The worst part was, she knew he wanted her, too. Desire burned in his eyes and sometimes radiated from every hard angle and plane of his body. But so far he had respected the subtle signals she sent him. Her body was primed for his, her heart ached for him, but her head cautioned her to watch her step.

Zach paused at the faucet just outside the barn to wash the sawdust from his hands. Ellie watched with fascination as he sluiced water first over his arms, then bent down to wash his shoulders, chest, and back. Finally he ducked his head under the flow, then turned off the tap and flung his head back, sending an arch of droplets in front of him.

He flashed her the devil's own grin when he caught her staring. "Mmm, that felt good," he said, blotting the excess water from his body with his shirt, which he then slung around his neck.

The barn's interior was bathed in the warm, incandescent glow from the incubator, inside of which twenty-two eggs waited to hatch. Most of them belonged to her various "investors," who had agreed to allow their eggs to hatch rather than sell them for a quick thousand. But a half dozen belonged to the Red Canyon.

Ellie wasn't expecting anything spectacular from the eggs, not just yet. True, exactly forty-two days had elapsed since the first eggs had gone in—the exact gestation period. But she had learned from the delayed breeding activities of the ostriches themselves that things didn't always go according to schedule. She wasn't even sure which of the eggs, if any, were fertile. So she wasn't prepared for Zach's excited yelp.

"Ellie, there's a hole in one of the eggs!"

She leaned over and peered through the glass, her face inches from his. "I'll be ding-busted, there sure is." She trembled with excitement. Their first hatchling. It was an important milestone.

"How long does it take?" Zach asked, his nose pressed up against the glass like a kid in a candy store.

"About twenty-four hours, sometimes more."

He gave a low whistle. "That's a long time. Are you planning to watch the whole process?"

She nodded. "I want to know if the chick gets into trouble. Sometimes they need help. But you don't have to stay," she added.

"I wouldn't miss it."

And so they watched and waited through the long afternoon and evening, pausing only long enough to gulp down sandwiches. Zach dragged the table he'd been working on into the barn so he could work while he kept Ellie company. Oddly enough, they never ran out of conversation.

Gradually the chick enlarged the hole with his beak in what seemed an agonizing process. Then the hole became a crack as the chick, breathing hard between bursts of effort, worked on making an escape hatch.

About midnight, Ellie remembered why Zach had come with her to the barn in the first place. "Didn't you say there was something you wanted to talk to me about?"

"Hmm?" Zach thought for a moment. "Oh, right. I almost forgot. Now I don't want you to make more of this than is warranted, but I've decided to take the Red Canyon off the market."

If anything could distract Ellie from her vigil over the egg, this was it. She turned to stare at him. "Are you serious?"

He tried to maintain an offhand manner, but she could tell he was ready to cut loose with a big smile. "Of course I am. I've talked it over with Jeff, and he thinks this place could be a very profitable investment, now that the cash flow is turning around."

"I've been telling you that from the start," she said indignantly.

"And you were right. So as long as the operation continues to grow and move toward profitability, I'll keep it."

He could clothe his decision with any logical, businesslike rationalization he wanted, Ellie mused, but in her mind it still added up to the same thing: he had finally committed himself to the Red Canyon. Did he have any idea how happy that made her?

"Oh, Zach, thank you." Although she longed to throw her arms around him and kiss him till his teeth rattled, she wouldn't repeat that mistake. Her gratitude, though overwhelming, wouldn't get out of hand this time. Instead she put her arm around his waist and gave him a friendly squeeze.

He slung his arm across her shoulders in an outward gesture of warm camaraderie. Inwardly Ellie struggled to maintain her composure as the embers of desire burst to life inside her. She forced herself to concentrate on the little miracle unfolding before them in the incubator.

"I wonder how they know when it's time to come out?" Zach asked at about 3:00 a.m., when Ellie returned from a brief nap. His voice was full of awe.

"I imagine they get kinda cramped," Ellie said through a yawn.

Soon they caught glimpses of bright shoe-button eyes and the damp, fuzzy feathers of the chick as it pushed against the shell and pecked at it some more. Shortly before noon, after what seemed an eternity, the baby ostrich finally broke free of its prison, then sat and took a well-deserved rest as its brown-striped body dried in the warm incubator.

Ellie had watched lots of chicken eggs hatch, but none of them had ever moved her the way this one did. She had a lump in her throat the size of a walnut.

"What do we do now?" Zach asked in a soft voice. He held her in a loose embrace, his fingertips unconsciously running up and down her ribs, lightly brushing the underside of her breast.

Somehow she managed a normal response. "We leave him in there for a while, then transfer him to the brooder and see if we can keep him alive. The chicks have a high mortality rate, you know."

"Don't say that," Zach admonished her. "I can tell this guy's going to make it. He looks like a strong, robust rooster to me."

"I suppose you're going to name it?"

"Yeah. I thought we'd call him Clem. What do you think?"

The lump in her throat grew to the size of a golf ball. "I think that's a wonderful idea," she said, her words barely above a whisper. The more she tried to swallow away the lump, the bigger it got. And there was no way she could stop the tears from streaming down her cheeks.

Before she knew what was happening, Zach was holding her, cradling her head against his shoulder, rubbing her back in slow, sensual circles. "Easy, honey. I didn't mean to make you sad. We can call the bird something else if you want."

"I'm not sad," she said. "Clem is a perfect name, and I think your uncle would be honored. If it turns out to be a hen, we can change it to Clementine."

Zach chuckled at that. "You really loved him, didn't you?"

Ellie nodded against Zach's chest. "He was like my second papa. I wish he could have been here to see this."

"Maybe he is here."

She cocked her head back to look at him. His face was so close to hers that she could feel his warm breath. "What do you mean?"

Zach shrugged. "I don't know. It's just that sometimes, even though I don't remember ever meeting the man, I feel like I know him."

"You would have liked him, Zach," she said as she ran her hands up and down the granite-hard muscles of his arms and shoulders. "He would have liked you, too." Then she added shyly, "I like you."

"Do you, now?" His eyes darkened with a suddenness that daunted her. "Then why do you work so hard at keeping your distance from me?"

So, he'd noticed her struggle with her hormones. "Maybe because I like you too much. And I'm afraid...."

"Afraid of what?" He nuzzled her ear, then her cheek, then the corner of her mouth, making it nearly impossible to think.

"I'm afraid of falling in love with you." She couldn't believe what she'd just blurted out. The lack of sleep had stolen all her inhibitions. "And you wouldn't want that, would you?"

He remained frighteningly silent as he prolonged his assault on her senses, planting a teasing chain of kisses down her neck.

"Well, *I* wouldn't want it," she continued, although by now her argument was a lost cause. "It's already tough enough saying goodbye to you every time you leave here. I'm not much for long-distance romance."

"Me, neither," he said in a husky voice as he unfastened the top button of her blue denim work shirt. "What's this thing you're wearing under your shirt?" He undid another button.

"It's an undershirt, and will you stick to the...uh... subject, please?" His clever fingers left trails of fire wherever he touched her, and she found it hard to breathe.

"What subject?" Her shirt was open to her waist. He pushed it off her shoulders, along with her white cotton undershirt, which was unadorned except for a narrow lace edging around the neckline. The undershirt caught on her upturned nipples. Zach seemed fascinated with the effect.

Ellie gave up. The red-hot desires rushing to overcome them had the power of a tidal wave. She couldn't fight them anymore. She didn't even want to. Hampered by the half-on, half-off shirt, she hugged him around his lean midsection, then kissed him full on the mouth with enough wattage to melt the sheet-metal barn.

It was Zach who finally broke the kiss, summoning some vestige of control. "Ellie," he said in a hoarse voice, "you do understand I'm not going to live here, right?"

She tamped down her disappointment. After all, he'd made a monumental step in the right direction by agreeing to keep the ranch. She couldn't expect him to leap the rest of the way all in one day. "I understand."

"Jeff does a great job handling things for me while I'm down here, but I can't neglect my business."

She nodded. "I know that. But as long as you own the place, you'll have to visit from time to time, to check on your investment, right?"

A slow smile spread across his face. "Probably every chance I get. I'm starting to like it down here." He paused to finger the lace edging of her undershirt, which was now bunched around her waist. "You like pretty underthings, don't you?"

Her face, already warm, suffused with more heat. "Surely I'm allowed one indulgence."

"Or two." He nipped at the tender flesh of her exposed breast, coming close to but not touching the nipple. "You know the real reason I've worked so hard fixing up the house?"

She thought she knew. But she wanted him to tell her. "No, why?"

"Because I had to keep my hands and my brain occupied every minute of the day. I worked until I was worn-out, so I wouldn't be tempted to..." He swore softly, so that the word had the effect of an endearment. "Ah, Ellie, let me make love to you."

Her breath felt trapped inside her chest. She couldn't think. She wasn't sure if she *wanted* to think, because if she did, she might find a reason to say no to Zach. And she wanted to say yes, very much. Hadn't they denied these feelings long enough?

"I'd like that," she heard herself saying.

In response he smoothed her undershirt over her breasts, settled the straps onto her shoulders, then swung her into his arms and carried her all the way back to the house.

Ellie seemed hardly a burden at all, Zach thought, as he managed to hook the screen-door handle with his elbow and swing it open. She weighed no more than feathers in his arms, and the way she clung to him so sweetly, planting nervous little kisses on his neck and around his ear, he was surprised he didn't just float back to her bedroom.

In the end, he never really remembered how they got there—just that Ellie was now lying across the Native American blanket she used as a bedspread while he unfastened the remaining buttons of her shirt and worked it off her body. Afternoon sunlight streamed through the open window along with a light breeze, spilling onto her golden skin, haloing her hair in reddish highlights. Ellie was by far the most naturally beautiful woman he'd ever seen, let alone touched.

Between them, hands impatient, they pulled off her boots and socks and jeans, until all that remained was that paper-thin undershirt and a matching set of French-cut panties. Given that everything else about her was so plain and practical, he never would have guessed she had a penchant for naughty underwear. That made him wonder what other little secrets she hid from him, secrets only a lover would know.

She reached for his belt, and he realized he'd been staring at her for a long time, mesmerized by the play of light and shadow across her skin, and the tantalizing view he had of dark areolas through thin white cotton.

He allowed her to unfasten his jeans, but, recognizing his own tenuous control, he pulled her hands away and finished the job himself, kicking off his boots and stripping out of his jeans and briefs in record time.

Ellie gave a throaty laugh and held her arms open, inviting him to join her on the bed. "I don't think I've ever seen a man get undressed that fast."

"I'm highly motivated," he said as he accepted her invitation. "How many men have you seen get undressed at all?"

"Not very many," she admitted.

For a few moments he was content just to hold her in his arms, exploring the enticing curves of her back and hips with the palms of his hands. She was everything a woman should be, soft in the right places, firm in others, smelling of sunshine and fresh mountain air, breathing new life into him when she kissed him. But Ellie, apparently, was not content. She wiggled and squirmed as he executed his exploration, igniting a fire in him big enough to consume them both. Soon her questing mouth found his, and he spent several minutes savoring the taste of desire on her.

As they kissed, he worked his hands beneath the undershirt to test the smoothness of her back, her trim waist, her soft, soft breasts. Although small, her breasts were perfectly shaped, with generous brown nipples that peaked at his touch. He brought one of them to his mouth, something he'd ached to do for a long time. She responded with a groan as her neat, practical fingernails raked trails across his shoulders.

"Zach..."

He looked up from where he'd been flicking his tongue over her navel while he stroked her thighs. He trailed one finger along the edge of her panties. "Want me to stop?"

"Yes! No... I mean..."

"My sentiments exactly." He whisked her panties down her legs and off, but he let her keep the undershirt. It was such a skimpy bit of fluff, revealing more than it hid, anyway.

Zach covered her body with his, but for a long time he just stared into Ellie's eyes, anticipating the moment of joining. Breathing in short, excited pants, she smiled shyly, then reached between their bodies to touch him.

The bold gesture surprised him. He closed his eyes and surrendered to her touch as she explored the length of him with tentative fingers.

"I've never wanted anybody like I want you," she said in a throaty whisper, as he fitted himself in the cradle of her parted thighs. Anticipation gave way to the thrill of possession as he entered her.

There was a certain rightness about the way she fit around him so snugly. For several heartbeats Zach didn't move, scarcely breathed. He was so intensely aroused that the slightest motion would have sent him over the edge. But soon he gathered a few shreds of control and he began to move, rocking gently at first, then more forcefully.

Sensations, hot and urgent, drove him. He buried his face against her neck, inhaling deeply the wondrous scent of her skin, feeling rather than hearing the small sounds of approval she made in the back of her throat as their sensual dance accelerated.

When she reached her peak, her eyes flew open and she cried out in surprise. That was all Zach needed. He let go of his rigid control and poured himself into her, all the while murmuring her name.

Afterward he felt dizzy. Worried that he might collapse on top of Ellie and crush her, he gently eased himself away from her, dropping a kiss on her dazed mouth before falling back to recover from the most delicious ordeal of his life.

"Zach?" Ellie whispered.

He realized then that he hadn't given her any of the reassurances a woman needs after the first time. He took her hand and brought it to his mouth. "What is it, honey?"

"Did I do okay?"

He chuckled and leaned on one elbow, so he could look into her eyes. They were like pools of liquid sky, shiny and overbright with unshed tears. "You did more than okay."

"I thought I knew what I was doing with this bedroom stuff, but you just blew me away." She looked down, her lashes casting elongated shadows.

He caressed her smooth cheek. "I'll take that as a compliment."

"How do you do it?"

"Do what?"

"You know just where to kiss, where to touch, even what to say. Does it take a lot of practice?"

Her concern charmed him no end. "A little practice, maybe," he said modestly. "But mostly I think you have to be adventurous and follow your instincts. Try new things. Find out what pleases. For example..." He roused himself out of bed and went to her dresser, where the vase full of ostrich plumes sat. He plucked one of the huge feathers from the vase and returned to the bed as Ellie's eyes grew wide.

"What are you going to do with that?"

For an answer he brushed the tip of the feather in slow circles over her flat belly. "Do you like this?"

She sighed. "Goodness, yes." She giggled when he hit a ticklish spot, then grabbed the feather from his hand. "Let me try."

Tentatively she touched him with the plume, tracing his ribs, circling his nipples. Zach closed his eyes and reveled in the incredible effect.

"Hmm, I don't know," she said. "I'm afraid I'll never be a match for you."

He laughed again. "Ellie, honey, you're more than a match for me, in bed or out of it. Just look what you do to me."

Her gaze raked over his body. She couldn't possibly miss the evidence of his renewed desire. "Ohhhhh," she said, the single word brimming with possibilities.

A ringing phone dragged Ellie from her pleasant drowsing. Reluctantly she pushed herself into a sitting position and reached for the phone by the bed. She cleared her throat before answering, "Hello, Red Canyon," positive the person on the other end would know what she'd been up to.

"Hello, Ellie, this is Phyllis Quincy. Is Zach Shaner there? His business partner in St. Louis told me he was visiting Rocky Ridge." She put an emphasis on the word *visiting*.

Ellie looked down at Zach, who was sound asleep, his tanned face contrasting pleasantly with the white eyelet pillowcase. "Is it all right if he calls you back?" She didn't even attempt to manufacture an excuse.

"Well, it is rather important, but I guess it's all right. I'll be at the office until five at least. He has the number." She hung up.

Ellie let the receiver fall to its cradle. There could be only one reason for the witch to call, and that would be to renew her offer to buy the Red Canyon.

The lightness in Ellie's heart disappeared, replaced by a bad case of the nervous flutters. Now why was she worried? Zach had taken the ranch off the market, right? But his reasons were practical ones. And he hadn't promised he wouldn't change his mind.

Ten

Ellie was tempted to let Zach sleep. He looked so appealing, so vulnerable, with his hair tousled like a little boy's. She wanted to curl up next to him again and drowse with his reassuring warmth surrounding her. But there was work to be done . . . and phone calls to be returned.

She gently shook his shoulder. "Zach, wake up."

"Hmm?" He rolled over and offered her a lazy smile. "Morning already?"

"It's four o'clock in the afternoon. You've got a table to refinish, and I have a garden to weed. We lost a whole day watching that silly chick hatch. Oh, and Phyllis Quincy called," she added offhandedly. "She wants you to call her at her office before five."

To her relief Zach appeared only mildly curious. "Wonder what she wants?" he asked, as he pulled himself out of bed. Although Ellie had already showered and dressed, deliberately distancing herself from the lovemaking so she could get her head out of the clouds, Zach was no more self-conscious about his lack of clothing than Ben Poteet's yellow tomcat.

Then again, he had nothing to be embarrassed about, she thought, as she watched him walk out the door and across the hall. His was a magnificent specimen of healthy male anatomy. She couldn't help but remember how reassuringly firm his body had felt to her touch, firm yet responsive. Inwardly she sighed, wondering what his thoughts were, if he'd been as profoundly affected by their lovemaking as she, if he wanted to repeat it.

Did he plan on sleeping in her bed tonight? Should she invite him to? She simply wasn't well versed in sex etiquette.

Zach waited until he was out of the shower and dressed to return Phyllis's call. When he did, he used the office phone, but he left the door open. As Ellie assembled the ingredients for their dinner that night, she couldn't help but overhear his side of the conversation.

"I'm sorry, Phyllis, but the answer's still no. The Red Canyon is going to make me a lot of money over the next few years and hopefully into the next century. To sell it would be like killing the ostrich that laid the thousand-dollar eggs, if you'll pardon my literary license."

Ellie's heart soared. Obviously Phyllis had renewed her offer to buy, and Zach was turning her down flat. He really was committed!

"Chicken again tonight?" he asked when he came into the kitchen.

"And tomorrow night, and the next," she said, fighting the urge to throw her arms around him and kiss him senseless. "In fact, you can count on it every night for some time to come. My folks decided they didn't want to wait for the next hog butchering to invest in a second egg, so they've been inundating us with chicken. I'm racking my brain for

new recipes. Do you have any idea how much chicken five
hundred dollars can buy?''

"That's okay, I like chicken. Um, listen, Ellie, I need to
go back home for a while.''

Her breath caught in her throat, fluttering like a wild bird
in a cage. The man had a nasty habit of giving with one
hand and taking away with the other. Or maybe he just had
excellent timing, delivering bad news when she was riding
high so it wouldn't hurt as much. "I'm not surprised," she
said mildly, amazed at how casual she sounded. "You've
spent so much time away from your business, your partner
must be ready to skin you alive.''

"Oh, I don't know. I think he enjoys running the show.
And I have to admit he's been doing a good job. But there
are some delicate negotiations coming up that demand my
attention. Can you handle things by yourself for a few
days?''

"Sure, no problem," she said with a carefree shrug intended to hide her inner turmoil. "I need to put a few hours
in on the chick pen, but Jimmy can help with that. He's doing some part-time work for Ben Poteet over the summer,
so he can come on over here in the afternoons.''

"Good. I'll leave you plenty of money so you can pay him
a fair salary. Speaking of salary, when are you going to start
accepting one again?''

"When there's more to spare," she said easily as she
rolled dough for a fat dumpling between her hands. "The
ranch isn't exactly a raging profit maker yet. We're chop-
ping a dent in the debts, but we're a long way from operating in the black.''

Zach shook his head and rolled his eyes. This was a well-
worn argument, one he never was able to win. "You don't
act like any employee I've ever had. No demands for a raise
or increases in fringe benefits—''

"I've made all kinds of demands," she countered. And she was getting fringe benefits. Her face flushed with heat at the naughty thought.

"Not the usual demands. You act more like a partner than an employee. Maybe I should just make you a partner."

"Uh, that's really not necessary," she said as she accidentally flattened a dumpling into a pancake. There was only one way she would consider becoming Zach's partner, and that was a rather farfetched possibility.

"But it makes sense. I'm sure Clem meant for you to have the Red Canyon when he died. It should be yours."

She grew very still inside. He appeared to be serious about this new idea of his. "It doesn't matter who owns it," she said in an unsteady voice, "so long as someone keeps the dream alive."

"That someone should be you. Maybe now that the ranch is earning some money, the bank would let me sign over half ownership to you. I'll look into it."

The tightness in her chest increased. She didn't want to tie Zach to her in any business sense, not when their personal relationship was on such unsteady footing. She chose her next words carefully. "It's not that I'm ungrateful, Zach, but I don't think our being partners is such a good idea. I like being an employee. Actually owning a ranch might be too much for me. I've never owned anything in my life."

His expression told her he wasn't buying.

"Besides," she added, "if I owned half the Red Canyon, you'd never be able to sell it, if that's what you were inclined to do."

He seemed to consider her point, then didn't challenge her further. Perhaps he wasn't as committed as she'd hoped.

Several times during the course of the past hour, Zach had been forced to drag his concentration back to his meeting with the Wysocki brothers, two intense young men with a good idea on their hands and no money to make it work.

He and Jeff sat with the brothers around a glossy walnut conference table. Zach, feeling oddly uncomfortable in his custom-tailored summer suit, watched detachedly as Jeff crunched numbers as fast as his calculator would take them.

At one time Zach had truly enjoyed this sort of high-pressure meeting. Now all he could think about was getting out of this climate-controlled prison and getting into his jeans and boots. His mind filled with visions of sun-dappled mountain vistas, the feel of smooth wood and the sun warming his back...the feel of Ellie's silky skin beneath his hands....

"Zach?"

Ah, hell, he was doing it again. "I'm sorry. My mind keeps rushing ahead to the bottom line," he said, improvising. "Let's go over those accounts-receivable figures again."

When the meeting was over, Jeff followed Zach into his office. "So, what do you think?"

"It's a big step for us," Zach replied. "Providing venture capital is a helluva lot riskier than merely consulting."

"Yeah, but who better to evaluate the risks of a start-up business than us? We've seen zillions of businesses fail and the steps that brought them there. Besides, we've got the money."

"That we do."

"So, what did you think?"

Zach shrugged. "The numbers add up. They've got a fresh idea in a growth service industry. It ought to pay off."

"I know that. But what do you think on a...you know, a gut level? Do you trust the Wysockis? That's why I wanted you here." Jeff paced nervously as he talked, his tortoise-shell glasses sliding down his nose again and again. "I can crunch numbers and read reports as well as anyone, but you're the one with the people instincts. You know as well as I do that it's the people behind a great idea that make things work."

That made him think of Ellie again. She was a remarkable woman behind a half-crazy idea, and she was making it work.

"Zach?" Jeff paused and stared at his partner.

"They seem like okay guys to me." That was the best Zach could do. Truthfully, he hadn't devoted enough attention to the subtle hints, like tone of voice, eye contact and body language, to make a valid judgment. Then again, nothing overtly negative had struck him.

Jeff sank into the chair across the desk from Zach. "Why do I get the feeling you're not quite all here?"

"Because I'm not. I can't get my mind off that damn ranch."

Jeff gave a snort of disgust. "Well, I wish you'd quit worrying about it. From everything you've told me, the potential yield is incredible. You've got a competent manager who knows more about the business than you do. Let her do the worrying."

How could Zach tell Jeff that Ellie was what he worried about most? She'd become an addiction for him. Making love to her hadn't solved anything; it had only made him crave her to a sharper degree. Now that he knew the profound satisfaction of loving her, as well as the emotional high she shot into his system any time of the day or night he was with her, he thought of little else. He had never before let anything distract him from his work. *That's* what worried him.

His intercom buzzed. He pressed a button on his phone to open the channel. "Yes, Debbie."

"Ellie Kessler's on line two for you, Zach."

Ellie? He'd just talked to her last night, and she'd *never* call him at work. "I'll take it," he told his secretary as he grabbed the receiver and jabbed the appropriate button on the phone. "Ellie? Are you all right?"

There was a long pause before she answered. "No, Zach, I'm not all right." Her voice was just shy of hysterical. "Two more chicks started hatching last night. There was a storm, and a power failure...I slept through the whole thing. The incubator was off for hours before I got the emergency generator started. I...I lost one of the chicks, and the eggs might be in trouble."

Zach gulped at the news. If his math was correct, at least nineteen unhatched eggs were involved. But what really concerned him was Ellie's distress. She had invested so much of her emotions into this operation. He found himself wanting to make everything right—not so much to protect his investment, but to comfort his woman.

His woman.

"There's more," she said. "I don't want to go into all the gory details now but...well, I know you're busy, but as soon as you can get away, I really need you, Zach."

"I'll be there by this evening," he said without hesitation. If Ellie said she needed help, she needed help. After a few more words of reassurance he hung up, then turned to his partner. "Jeff, is the plane available for the next couple of days?"

Jeff was staring at him, his mouth gaping open. "You're leaving? How can you pick up and leave in the middle of—"

"I don't have any choice. It's an emergency."

Jeff sighed. "Yeah, the plane's yours. But something tells me there's a little more than business involved in this ranch of yours. If this were an ordinary investment, or a client, you would at least try to handle it on the phone first—whatever the problem."

Jeff was right, Zach thought guiltily. A helluva lot more than business was involved. But after spending so much time with Ellie, he found he had rearranged his priorities. There were more important things in life than making a sound, rational business decision.

"You can handle the Wysockis," Zach said. In the back of his mind, he knew he ought to stick around for the consummation of this deal. Just the same, his feet carried him to his car, and his car took him straight to the airport.

As Zach climbed down from the Piper Cub, still in his suit pants and crisply starched white shirt, Ellie had never been so grateful for the sight of another human being in her life. With absolutely no shame she ran toward him and threw herself into his arms and sobbed against his shoulder. "Oh, Zach, I'm so glad you're here. Everything's falling apart."

He wrapped his arms around her in a welcoming hug. "Easy, honey. It can't be as bad as all that. We'll sort things out one step at a time. Here, give me the keys. I'll drive."

"Where's your bag?" she asked, pulling herself together with no small effort.

"I didn't stop to pack one. It's okay. I left some things at the ranch. Now, why don't you start at the beginning?"

As Zach negotiated the unwieldy truck through winding roads, Ellie pointed out the worst of the damage, though most of it was obvious. Broken branches littered the road, and even a few larger trees had been felled by the high winds.

"Did the house or the barn sustain any damage?" he asked.

She nodded grimly. "The house is fine, but the wind took half the roof off the barn. Almost all the feed is ruined."

"If feed's all we lost, that's not hard to replace," Zach said with a reassuring smile. "And the barn needed a new roof anyway. What else?"

"The birds themselves are so upset I didn't find any eggs this morning. There probably won't be any more for a few days."

"That's okay. I'm sure they'll start laying again once they settle down."

Ellie shrugged. "Even if they do, there's another problem. Duane Scoggins won't be buying any more Red Canyon eggs for a while. Says he's got more stock than he needs right now, and he's having a cash-flow problem or some such nonsense."

"So we'll start incubating more eggs. We can get an even better price for chicks, right?"

"Tell that to the shareholders. They want to see a return on their investment *now*, not in two months or more. I might be able to find a buyer for the chicks once they're a few weeks old, but we'll have to get by without any income for a while."

"You should be used to no income by now," he teased.

She tried, but she couldn't come up with a smile for him. She found it ironic that their roles had reversed. He was the hopeful one, she the pessimist. But that was because he didn't know the worst of it yet. She was having a hard time getting the bad news past her constricted throat.

"Ellie, come on. You never once lost your optimism during those gloomy weeks when the ostriches weren't laying eggs and the bills were piling up. Why now?"

"Because... because the bank's calling in its loan."

Zach was silent for a long, scary minute. The only sign she had that her words had reached his brain was the small muscle that twitched in his jaw. "Which loan?" he finally asked.

She sighed. "The big one."

"Damn."

"Can they do that?" she asked.

"I won't know till I read the loan papers, but since there were several late payments last spring, my guess is they have a perfectly legal right. My question is, why now? We're caught up, right?"

"The last two payments have been right on time," Ellie confirmed. "And I can tell you 'why now' in one word—SunnyLand."

"Oh, you don't really think...do you?"

"What happens if we can't come up with the money?"

"The bank forecloses," Zach replied.

"And what's a bank going to do with an ostrich ranch?"

The conclusion was inescapable. "Sell it to SunnyLand. You may be right. But I still have a hard time imagining that Phyllis Quincy could be so ruthless as to encourage the bank to force our hand."

Ellie didn't find it hard at all. "Well, you'll finally get your wish," she said.

"What wish?"

"You'll be rid of the Red Canyon."

"Like hell!" The violence of his reaction reverberated in the closed truck cab. Then he took her hand and squeezed it in silent apology for the outburst. "Ellie, honey, the bank's not going to get the Red Canyon, and neither is SunnyLand, not if I can help it."

For the first time since she'd awakened that morning to find her world upside-down, Ellie felt hopeful. She didn't have to face her problems alone, not anymore. And if anyone could figure a way out of this mess, Zach could. That's what he did for a living, after all, wasn't it? He kept businesses from going bankrupt.

As Zach pulled the truck into the driveway, he began to realize the full extent of the storm damage. No wonder Ellie was upset. Debris of every description, from branches to beer cans, littered the yard and pastures, blown in from who knew where. A fifty-foot section of fence was down, although thankfully there had been no birds in that pasture. The garden was flattened. And the barn—the barn looked like a giant had taken a can opener to it.

After looking in on the two surviving chicks, which appeared healthy and active and oblivious to this new threat to their future, Zach went inside to ferret out the mortgage papers from a rusty file cabinet. He was even more discouraged after reviewing the terms. The bank, a small institution in nearby Jasper, was well within its rights in calling in the loan. He had thirty days to come up with the cash, or the bank would begin foreclosure proceedings. He knew of only one place he could get his hands on that much money.

Zach waited until Ellie was busy elsewhere before placing the call to Jeff. "Hey, buddy, how do you feel about Shaner-Hodges, Inc., investing in an ostrich ranch?" he asked his partner.

"Are things that bad?"

"Things are worse than bad." He started to explain the situation, but Jeff interrupted.

"Whoa, wait a minute. You can save your breath. Even if this place is the investment of the century, it's a no-go. Shaner-Hodges, Inc., doesn't have the money to invest in a gum-ball machine right now."

"What? What are you talking about?"

"The Wysocki brothers, remember? You told me to handle it, and I did. I wrote the check out not half an hour ago."

"Oh, hell." So much for the company's venture-capital budget. Of all the rotten timing.

After ending his conversation with Jeff, Zach went to the kitchen and poured himself some lemonade, racking his brain for some other source of capital. It was too damn bad his trust fund was beyond his reach, but he didn't turn thirty for another nine months, and there was no way his tight-fisted trustee, an old friend of his father's, would let go of a single nickel before it was time.

The way Zach saw it, he had two choices. He could accept SunnyLand's offer and get some money out of the deal. Or he could let the bank foreclose, ruin his credit rating and come away with nothing. At this point the money meant little, and he was tempted to hold out just to get on Phyllis Quincy's nerves. She probably imagined she had him pinned neatly, now that she'd gotten the bank to cooperate with her scheme.

Ellie returned from the garden, her arms full of half-ripe tomatoes. "There must have been some hail," she said as she dumped the pitiful-looking crop onto the kitchen counter. "I saved these, at least. They'll ripen if we set them on the windowsill. But I'm afraid we lost more than we— Zach, what's wrong?"

There was no point in keeping the truth from her. "Ellie, I'm sorry."

Their gazes locked for several heartbeats before understanding dawned. She shook her head in denial as tears pooled in her blue eyes, making them appear even larger and darker than they were.

"I thought I could come charging down here like Superman and save the day," Zach said. "If there was any way I could see to come up with that money, you know I would, but... I'm sorry I got your hopes up."

When she said nothing, he felt compelled to fill the silence with words, meaningless words. "With the money I get from SunnyLand, I could set up a new operation somewhere. Maybe not as big, but we can keep the birds and..." Even he knew how impractical his plans sounded. You couldn't just pick up an ostrich farm and move it. Anyway, Ellie wasn't interested in another farm in another location. For her, it was the Red Canyon or nothing.

"They'll see it as a failure," she murmured.

"What?"

"The people on Rocky Ridge. If you sell to SunnyLand, they'll know we couldn't make it. It wouldn't matter if we set up somewhere else, even close by. No one will have faith in the plan anymore if the Red Canyon folds."

He heard more than disappointment in her words, saw more than sadness in her eyes. He could actually feel her sense of betrayal, like a physical wave rolling off her.

Never in all his years had he felt so helpless. He didn't know what to do next. So he did what came naturally, which was to reach for Ellie and enfold her in a hug.

She didn't resist, but neither did she accept his comfort. She stood stiffly in his arms, as inanimate as one of those broken branches that littered the yard. Even as his body responded to her nearness, her scent, her very essence, she retreated, in her mind if not physically.

The implications were plain. Not only was he losing the ranch, he was losing the one woman in his life who had ever meant something to him. But it appeared their relationship was inextricably tied to the success of the ranch. If he lost the Red Canyon, he lost Ellie, too.

They ought to be supplying comfort to each other now, when their carefully laid plans were falling apart. *Their* plans, *their* future. Losing the ranch wasn't just Ellie's loss. He had come to share her crazy dream, to invest hope and faith into it just as she had. It tore him up to think about bulldozers laying waste to the home he had fixed up, the fences he'd painted, the garden he and Ellie had planted together. But she wasn't going to allow him to share in her sadness. It seemed he was doomed to play the villain in this melodrama.

That isn't fair, a silent voice screamed inside his head. Whether she meant to do it or not, she was perpetrating a form of emotional blackmail, using the considerable hold she had on him to force him to make some decision other than the one he'd made. Didn't she understand that there was no other door open to him?

He stroked her hair, softening toward her. Maybe, he thought, she simply couldn't feel close to him when she was so adamantly opposed to his actions. In time she might come to understand, and they would be close again. It was the first time he had admitted to himself that he wanted some sort of future with Ellie, apart from the Red Canyon.

But enough of this sentimentality. He was a businessman, and there were decisions to be made. Hardening his heart, he pushed her gently away from him. "I'll have to get the sale moving along if we want to avoid foreclosure," he said. "I can postpone the date SunnyLand takes possession of the property, but not for long. We'd better see what we can do about arranging for the birds to be transferred to their new home."

He half expected her to balk, to become angry as she had the last time they'd talked about selling the ranch. But instead she shored herself up and looked him in the eye, almost as if to prove she could be just as detached as he. "Okay. They're going to the Deever farm, right?" she asked, referring to the ostrich farm a hundred miles away where SunnyLand had arranged to sell the Red Canyon's birds.

"Yes, that's right."

"What about the eggs and the chicks?" she asked.

"Those aren't included in the deal," he said. "We'll have to make our own arrangements. Is there any way to transport incubating eggs?"

"I don't know. I'll look into it." She turned and left him without another word, going into the office. The only indication of the true state of her feelings was the way she slammed the door.

Later that night, as he lay alone in his bed, sleepless and cold despite the summer heat, a revelation struck Zach in the

forehead as surely as a mule's rear hooves. What was wrong
with him? He was renowned throughout the St. Louis financial community as the man who could snatch a floun-
dering business from the jaws of bankruptcy. When
everyone else had written off the business as a lost cause,
Zach was the man who came up with the creative solution,
the methods that hadn't occurred to anyone else. Yet when
it came to the Red Canyon, he hadn't been able to see past
that notice from the bank, that incredible hunk of money
that couldn't possibly be raised in a month's time. Everything appeared black-and-white.

But maybe, just maybe, his mind was playing a trick on
him, hiding any possible solutions to the problem. The truth
was, he was afraid to commit one hundred percent of himself to the ranch, which he would have to do if he came up
with any plan to save it.

There was so much more involved here than a simple
business decision. Whatever he did with the Red Canyon, it
would affect the rest of his life.

What did he want? Where were his priorities?

As if in answer to his mental question, a flood tide of
ideas flowed through his consciousness. He could go to another bank—maybe one in St. Louis, where he knew the
personnel. He could convince them the Red Canyon was a
good risk and get another loan. Although he couldn't touch
his trust fund, maybe he could use it as collateral.

Or he could sell some of the flock and pay off the mortgage that way. Hadn't Ellie told him he owned almost half
a million dollars' worth of "feathers on the hoof"? Although she had preconceived notions about how many birds
she needed to make the operation succeed on a grand scale,
there was no law that said they couldn't scale down for a
while. Perhaps he could even work out a new deal with
SunnyLand and sell them only part of the land they wanted.
The Red Canyon had several empty pastures, after all.

The ideas bombarded his brain, keeping him up half the night. He had to fight the urge to walk to the other side of the house, wake Ellie and tell her.

But he couldn't tell her, he realized. What if none of his ideas panned out? What if he only *thought* he could save the ranch? He couldn't bear to disappoint her again.

Eleven

When Ellie awoke the next morning, her head ached from
unshed tears, and her heart felt like an anvil inside her chest.
But she was determined not to cry anymore. Crying was for
quitters, and she was a survivor. She threw back the covers
and climbed out of bed. Coffee sounded like a good idea.

She paused in the hallway when she smelled the unmis-
takable scent of bacon coming from the kitchen. Zach
wasn't usually up this early, and he hardly ever made
breakfast. Was he trying to butter her up? Did he think any
food, no matter how delicious, could make up for the fact
that he was tearing her whole world down piece by piece?

She tightened the sash around her robe, readying herself
for an argument. But before she even set foot in the kitchen,
the fight seeped out of her. She was so desolate she couldn't
even get up a good head of steam. It took too much energy
to lose her temper, and besides, she wasn't so much angry
at Zach as supremely disappointed in him. Obviously he

wasn't as committed to the ostrich operation as he'd led her to believe. If he were, if he had truly come to love the land and its people...and her...he would move heaven and earth to save this place. But he was still thinking in terms of dollars and cents.

And speaking of dollars and cents, what about that zillion-dollar trust fund of his? But desperate as she was for a solution, she hesitated to make the suggestion. That money was Zach's legacy from his father. She couldn't expect him to pledge it to such a risky venture, not when he didn't believe in it.

She entered the kitchen, her head held high and her chin thrust forward in determination. Zach stood at the stove with his back to her. A sky blue T-shirt stretched across his shoulders, and his faded jeans rode low on his narrow hips. His hair was still damp from a morning shower, and the ends curled a bit.

Even after all that had happened, she longed to wrap her arms around him and kiss the back of his neck, to lose herself in the fire of his touch, the mindless ecstasy of his lovemaking. But that would be a senseless, self-indulgent weakness. He would soon be gone from her life, or what was left of it. It would be hard enough adjusting to his absence. No, now that there were barriers erected between them, she'd best leave them up.

He must have heard her as she hovered near the kitchen table, unsure whether she wanted to sit down, because he turned and offered her a cautious smile. "'Morning. Coffee's ready. And I'm making bacon and eggs."

She gave him a sour look. "I'll take the coffee, but *eggs?* How could you?"

"Sorry. I would have opted for pancakes, but I always burn them."

"Never mind, I'm really not hungry." She poured herself a mugful of coffee and retreated quickly to her bedroom to dress. She didn't trust herself in the same room with him, not when her feelings were so near the surface.

Indifferently she threw on her oldest jeans and an over-size T-shirt, then ran a brush through her hair. She couldn't find an elastic band, so she left her hair loose. By the time she came out again, Zach was in the office with the door closed—hiding from her, she imagined. And could she blame him? She hadn't exactly been Miss Congeniality.

With a sigh, she refilled her coffee cup. She could hear the muffled sound of Zach's voice as he spoke on the phone. She wondered who was on the other end of the line.

By noon Zach had a plan, and it was so simple he couldn't imagine why he hadn't thought of it in the first place. The trick was to carry it out without clueing Ellie in. He didn't want her to even suspect what he was up to.

The first step was the one he dreaded the most. He had to ask Ellie to drive him to the airstrip. He would be gone only a day, but he felt like he was abandoning her at a time when she shouldn't be left alone. Then again, at this point she might be relieved to be rid of him. He was hardly her knight in shining armor.

He found her in the pasture with the young ostriches, feeding them lettuce. For a long time he simply watched her, struck anew by how beautiful she was, lithe and graceful among the gawky birds. The sun shone on her fresh face, and the wind blew her hair into a tangled halo. She crooned to the birds as she coaxed them to eat from her hand, and he got the uncomfortable feeling that she was saying good-bye to them. She claimed not to have any sentimental at-tachment to the silly beasts, but her actions said otherwise.

He didn't know how long he might have stood there, drinking in the sight of her. But something else caught his attention. A lone rooster, the only mature bird in the lot, stood separated from the main group. Its attention was focused on Ellie as it puffed out its feathers in a now-familiar show of aggression.

Zach's heart rose to his throat. Ellie didn't see the threat. "Ellie!" he called to her. But the wind carried his words away. Issuing a string of expletives, he was over the fence in an instant and running toward her as fast as his legs would take him. As he continued to yell out Ellie's name, he could only hope that his actions wouldn't make the rooster even madder.

Ellie's head jerked around when Zach got close enough that she could hear him. Her jaw dropped and her eyes widened, until he pointed in the direction of the angry ostrich. Immediately she understood. She dropped the lettuce and broke into a dead run. They both reached the fence at the same time. He worried for an instant that Ellie wouldn't get over in time, but she scaled the six-foot barrier with the agility of a monkey and beat him to the ground on the other side. The ostrich trailed them by only a few feet.

They stood catching their breaths for several seconds before Ellie looked at Zach. "Thank you. I think you just saved my life."

"No problem. What the hell is wrong with that bird? He's never done that before."

"They usually only act like that when they're breeding...wait a minute." She quickly counted heads in the herd. "Aha, one of the hens is missing, and I'll lay you ten-to-one odds it's his mate."

Zach scanned the pasture. The birds had grazed or trampled most of it down, but there were some tall weeds between the shelter and the fence that had been neglected. "Maybe she's hiding over there," he said, pointing to the weeds.

Ellie nodded, and they went to investigate. Sure enough, they found the fugitive hen—sitting on a nest close to the fence.

"Well I'll be damned," Ellie said softly. "That bird's only two years old. She's too young to breed."

"She apparently thinks otherwise."

Their talking disturbed the hen. She galumphed to her feet and walked away in a huff, revealing four eggs in the nest.

Zach laughed. "I guess this pair decided to buck the system and raise a clutch of babies on their own."

But Ellie wasn't laughing. She stared at the eggs, eyes transfixed, utterly still.

"How do you suggest we get them out of there? I might be able to cut a small hole in the fence and just reach through and—"

"Leave them," she said.

"What?"

"We both know she won't get to hatch those babies. The bulldozers will be here before that can happen. But let's let her have her illusions for a few more days. Four eggs don't mean much to us, not anymore, but they mean something to her."

That's four thousand dollars lying in that nest! Zach almost said. But he stopped himself in time. This wasn't about money. In some crazy way Ellie identified with these two misguided birds. They would never see their eggs hatch. She would never see her dream come to pass. Or so she thought.

He wanted to tell her not to give up, that he had a plan. But the plan was far from foolproof. If he got her hopes up again and then dashed them, it might break her spirit for good.

Ellie sniffled, and Zach realized she was crying.

"Oh, Ellie, don't cry."

She whirled around to face him. "Well, what am I supposed to do?" she demanded, her tear-streaked face a mask of defiance. "I'm sorry I can't deal with this the way you do, like it's just another business transaction."

"That's not how I feel at all. Ellie..." He touched her shoulder, but she sidestepped, avoiding his hand.

"Don't. I don't need your comfort." She turned and ran.

Damn, he couldn't leave the ranch now, not with Ellie in such a state. He followed her, slowly, giving her time to compose herself. But he had to confront her, to convince her that he did care, about the ranch, about her dreams, about her.

Ellie resisted the urge to run to the shelter of her room, lock the door, flop down on the bed and cry her heart out. Instead she forced herself to go to the barn and check on the chicks. If she could lose herself in work, in the everyday chores that had made up her days for the past three years, maybe she could convince herself that everything was normal—at least until Zach was gone.

And he would be gone, soon. She didn't need his help tending the birds these last few days, and his continued presence was only causing her pain. Surely he could see that. He should just sign those papers from SunnyLand and get the hell out of here. Then she could quietly fall apart, with no one to witness her indignity except the featherbrained birds.

The chicks looked hale and hearty. She took the larger one, the one Zach had named Clem, out of the brooder and held its fuzzy, squirming body close to her, taking comfort from its warmth and sheer vitality.

A soft footfall behind her alerted her to Zach's presence. Dammit, why couldn't he leave her alone? She quickly returned the chick to the brooder. "Why are you wearing those damn tennis shoes?" she asked instead. "At least with boots, you can't sneak up on a body."

"I left the boots in St. Louis. Didn't have time to pack, remember?"

"A lot of good it did for you to rush to the rescue."

"I did what I could."

"Yeah? Well, it wasn't enough, was it? I wish you hadn't come. I wish you'd *never* come here, Zach Shaner. I wish that probate lawyer'd never found you."

She turned then and saw him standing there in a shaft of sunlight that poured through the hole in the roof, looking like a pagan sun god. A tortured god. And it was her words that had brought that stark pain to his face. She could have bitten her tongue out. She didn't mean it, not a word of it.

He swiveled on one heel and stalked out of the barn.

She ran after him. By the time she caught up with him, he had stopped on the bluff that overlooked the creek—the same spot where they'd kissed for the first time, she remembered. The memory of the optimism that had propelled her into his arms all those weeks ago was bittersweet.

An altogether different emotion pushed her now. "Zach, I'm so sorry. Honest, I didn't mean to say those things. They aren't true. You tried. You did more than anyone else would have."

"But it wasn't enough."

"I'm not blaming you."

"Aren't you?"

"I'm *trying* not to blame you," she amended.

Her honesty prompted a wistful smile from him. "Thank you for that anyway. Is there anything I can do to make this more tolerable for you, Ellie?" He ruffled her bangs.

"You could make love to me." The words rushed out of her mouth without any thought on her part, yet she didn't wish them back. Every cell in her body suddenly clamored for his body. And perhaps by sharing herself in this intimate way one last time, she could say goodbye and close the doors on a precious part of her life, a part she would remember always.

Staring up at him, waiting for an answer, she saw the banked passion in his eyes and knew he wanted her as much as she did him. But he wasn't a man who acted on impulse.

He directed his gaze toward the sky, then down to the toes of his running shoes—anywhere but at her.

"You asked me what you could do," she said. "I told you. Maybe I'm hoping some of your strength will rub off on me if I can just get close enough."

When he finally looked at her, his eyes were filled with naked need. He smoothed her hair against her neck. "You're stronger than any three women I know. I'm the one who's weak."

"You?"

"Because I can't turn you down."

"Zach, if you want to turn me down, then do it. I won't fall ap—"

He silenced her with a kiss, a hungry, searching kiss that reached down to her toes and sealed their fate. Her heart raced double time as reality sank in. She would have him again, once more. She vowed to remember every kiss, every murmured endearment, the exact feel of his body, his hands, against her skin. Her memories would have to feed her soul for a long time to come.

This time Zach didn't even bother with taking her inside. They fell where they stood, to the soft summer grass. The earth was warm, welcoming.

Ellie unbuttoned Zach's shirt, bestowing kisses to the skin she bared as each button gave way. The light dusting of hair on his chest shone gold now against his tanned skin. She let it tickle her nose as she breathed in the arousing scent of him, then moved downward to lightly nip his firm belly as she unzipped his jeans.

Zach groaned. She looked up to see him biting his lower lip, the perfect picture of agony.

"Should I stop?" she asked in all innocence, still unsure of her powers in this unfamiliar arena.

"Please, go on," he said, enunciating every word.

She did. Remembering what he'd told her about following her instincts, she bared every inch of him to the sun's warming rays, then poured out her feelings for him with her hands, her lips, her tongue, even her hair.

Zach stood as much as he could before reaching for her, pulling her still-clothed body against his to capture her mouth once again with his. "You're a damned quick study," he murmured into her hair. "You know, this could easily become a habit."

Yes! No, she quickly corrected herself. For so long she had hoped that the Red Canyon and Rocky Ridge would speak to his soul as it had to hers. But if this world didn't bring him satisfaction, if he couldn't willingly give up his life in St. Louis without regret, she didn't want him here, no matter how gratifying their lovemaking.

He deftly unbuttoned her shirt and slid it down her arms. Then he cupped her breasts through the plain white bra she wore. "No fancies today?"

"Those are luxuries, not for everyday."

"If you were mine, you'd wear them all the time."

Ellie refused to let his words fill her with hope. He hadn't meant anything by them. "I'm yours . . . for now," she said lightly.

Unlike the first time they'd come together, so full of joy and celebration, now there was a poignant sadness to their fevered caresses, as if they both knew it was the last time. Zach kissed her tenderly, almost reverently, as he removed the last of her clothing, baring parts of her body that rarely saw the sun.

When she would have lain down in the grass, he rolled onto his back, pulling her on top of him. "Your back is too smooth and pretty to put against this hard ground," he said.

The way he treated her so tenderly brought silly tears to her eyes. She quickly blinked them back. She wouldn't spoil this moment with maudlin sentiment. He would only worry that he'd hurt her, or some such nonsense.

"What now?" she asked in a husky voice.

He pulled her head down toward his, and the fall of her hair formed a screen, blocking out the sun. "Follow your instincts," he said just before their lips met once again.

She lost herself in the potency of the kiss and the feel of his chest hair against her sensitive breasts. Chills of excitement swept her body despite the heat of the day. Without really thinking about it, she straddled his hips, softly grazing the length of his arousal with the soft flesh between her legs.

Her unconscious teasing drove him wild, but she'd aroused herself to the same fever pitch of desire. Unable to postpone the consummation of their love a moment longer, she guided him home, taking him deeply inside her. With his hands to encourage her, she rode him like a wild stallion, excited beyond the scope of reason at the new sensations created by their reversed positions. She wanted to continue forever just like this, joined to Zach in a shared moment of ecstasy. For her the ride ended too soon as her whole body tensed in an uncontrollable spasm so pleasurable she thought she would lose her sanity.

Somehow, through the cotton batting that swathed her mind, she realized Zach had found his release, also. They lay together for long, breathless minutes, slicked with sweat, breathing in unison.

Already Ellie mourned for what they were giving up.

"You ever been to St. Louis?" Zach asked.

"No."

"You ever want to go?"

"To visit, maybe," she said, willing her body not to tremble. *Don't ask me,* she pleaded. Much as she loved him, she couldn't live in his world. To leave Rocky Ridge behind was unthinkable.

Perhaps he heard her, because he didn't ask.

They were scarcely dressed before Zach asked Ellie to drive him to the airstrip. "I know this isn't the best timing...."

She should have known he would do this. Didn't it fit his pattern? "No problem," she said, trying to sound unconcerned.

"It *is* a problem," he said. "I can see it in your eyes. I'll be back tomorrow, Ellie, I swear it."

"Don't come back on my account," she said, injecting a note of steel into her voice. "Oh, but I guess you still have to sign some papers, right?"

He swallowed. "Right."

Ellie felt a pang of joy as she watched another chick fight its way into the world. She tried to tell herself it didn't matter; the poor little creature would end up sold to another rancher. But something inside her couldn't help but rejoice at the evidence that nature knew what it was doing. This new little life forced Ellie to realize that, despite the gloomy-looking future, her own life wasn't going to hell in a hand basket; it was merely taking a new direction.

She held on to that optimism for all of five minutes, the time it took her to band the baby ostrich's leg and return to the office to write down the details of the new hatchling's birth in the Red Canyon's record book. But there was no record book. It hadn't occurred to her to ask Zach what he was taking back with him to St. Louis in an old duffel bag. Now she knew. He'd cleaned out the office.

"Well, he isn't wasting much time," she muttered as she scribbled down the information on a torn piece of notebook paper. Let Zach try and decipher it later when he sold the chick.

She wouldn't stick around to explain, she decided then and there. She couldn't stop Zach from tearing down the

Red Canyon, but that didn't mean she had to stand around and watch.

She glanced at her watch. Only four o'clock. She picked up the phone and dialed a number from memory.

"Ben?" she asked when her neighbor's familiar gravelly voice answered. "Is Jimmy working there today?"

"Shore is. You want I should fetch him?"

"No, that's okay. Just tell him to stop by the Red Canyon and pick me up on his way home."

"You going home for a visit?" Normally Ben wasn't nosy about other people's affairs, but perhaps the tone of Ellie's voice had alerted him to the fact that something was wrong.

"A long visit," she answered before hanging up. In fact, she would never go back to the Red Canyon if she could help it. Jimmy could take care of the birds for a day or two, until Zach returned. *If* he returned. After that, the ranch was Zach's problem.

Twelve

Zach was supremely confident as he walked into the First National Bank of Jasper the following afternoon. He had spent almost the entire night going over the Red Canyon's records and preparing a comprehensive financial statement, but the lack of sleep was worth it. The arsenal of facts and figures he held in the folder under his arm would convince any sane lender that the ranch was a growing, viable enterprise.

He had a list of options to present to Wilford Bates, the loan officer. Zach's first choice would be for Bates to forget calling in the loan and for business to go on as usual. If that didn't appeal to him, Zach had a schedule of accelerated payments to present. Third choice was to negotiate a new loan at a higher interest rate.

Zach's final option would be to take his business to another lender. A banker friend in St. Louis had assured Zach that, with his background, he would have no trouble securing the loan. Surely Wilford Bates would see the wisdom of cooperating, when he realized he might lose the Red Canyon's business altogether, as well as the opportunity to sell to SunnyLand.

Wilford Bates, a thin, balding man who squinted through thick glasses, greeted Zach with formal courtesy. But as the little man ushered Zach into his office, Zach read his conflicting body language in an instant. Bates was nervous.

"I don't quite understand," Zach said after some initial posturing and throat clearing from both parties. "Why exactly are you calling in the loan *now,* when the last few payments have been prompt?"

Bates adjusted his glasses and stared out the window. "The trustees of this bank feel that the speculative nature of the Red Canyon's operation is not a good risk in today's market," he said in what was obviously a well-rehearsed speech. "The board recommended, and I concur, that we cut our losses now, foreclose on the property if necessary and sell while we have a buyer. As you are probably aware, SunnyLand, Inc.—"

"I know all about SunnyLand."

"Yes, well, you see, on down the road, that buyer will undoubtedly have purchased property elsewhere, and by then there might not be anything left of the Red Canyon to collect."

"What if I could convince you that the ostrich operation is a good risk?"

Bates shook his head without even considering the question. "Judging from the recent financial performance of the Shaner estate, I really don't think—"

"But things have changed," Zach insisted. "The ranch is averaging a gross income of two to three thousand dollars *per day.* You can't ignore those numbers."

"I'm not ignorant of the ins and outs of ostrich farming, Mr. Shaner," Bates said condescendingly, removing his glasses and polishing them with a handkerchief. "As a matter of fact, this bank does a lot of business with the

Deever farm. You're familiar with that operation, I'm sure.
And I've learned that an ostrich hen's productivity is a very
precarious thing."

"Yes, but—"

"And when the breeding season's over, where's your income?"

"We have twelve head of emu—"

"Immature, unproven birds, as I understand it."

This wasn't going at all as Zach had planned. Bates wasn't
even willing to look over the financial statement. He wasn't
amenable to a fresh loan. He wavered only slightly when
Zach mentioned refinancing at another bank, but then stood
firm. Unfamiliar with Zach's reputation in St. Louis, he
probably figured another bank wouldn't give him the time
of day, especially with the Red Canyon's dubious credit
rating.

Zach had no other choice but to pull out the big guns.
"Would two million dollars in collateral be enough to convince you that the loan is utterly secure?" he asked.

Bates blinked owlishly a couple of times. "You don't have
that kind of—"

"Yes, I do. I have a trust fund that comes under my control in less than nine months. My trustee has agreed to let me
use the fund now as collateral. I have all the necessary documentation—"

Bates shook his head. "There's no point in continuing this
discussion, Mr. Shaner. My mind's made up on this matter."

Again Zach noticed the evidence of Bates's nerves—a little tick in his cheek, the fine sheen of perspiration on his
balding pate. Running on nothing but guts and adrenaline,
Zach made his next move. "So, Wilford, that must be a
pretty healthy kickback you're getting from SunnyLand."

"I beg your pardon?" Bates was the picture of outrage,
but Zach saw through the bluster. The man was terrified.

Zach's instincts were on the money. Phyllis Quincy had bribed Bates to call in the loan.

"I can't think of any other reason you would deliberately turn away the opportunity to lend risk-free money at an attractive interest rate. I'll bet a bank examiner would be fascinated with your explanation."

Mr. Wilford Bates's demeanor changed abruptly. "Er, perhaps I've been a little hasty...."

Wearing heavy work boots, cut-off jeans, and a 1982 Oklahoma State Fair T-shirt, Ellie dumped a load of table scraps into the hog trough. The overfed hog lifted its head, sniffed the air, then hoisted itself from its mud bath to check out the snack.

"What a rough life you lead," Ellie said to the hog, which looked more like a baby hippopotamus than anything porcine. "Eating and lying in the mud—that's all you have to think about." Of course, being a hog had its drawbacks, namely the fact that in another couple of months the animal would become ham, bacon and pork chops. Ellie patted the poor thing on its broad head before heading back to the house.

She had sought refuge here, her childhood home, only to discover that she no longer belonged. Her parents had assured Ellie that she was welcome for as long as it took her to pull herself together and make some decisions. But she was uncomfortable with their unasked questions. Worse by far was their bland acceptance of this wretched turn of events. Nothing else had ever panned out for them, her father maintained; why should ostrich ranching be any different?

She'd given it her best shot, but the fact that she'd disappointed them, and all of Rocky Ridge, ate away at her conscience.

As she hung the empty bucket on the screened-in back porch and wiped her boots on the mat, her brother Jimmy

came barreling out the door, all six foot three of him.
Judging from the filthy state of his baseball uniform, he'd
had an active day at the ballpark.

"Hey, El. I did all the chores on the Red Canyon like you
told me. Everything's fine, but there're still no eggs."

"Thanks, Jimmy."

Hesitantly he asked, "Have you figured out how to come
up with the money yet?"

She shook her head. "There's no way," she said, flop-
ping onto a decrepit porch swing. "Everybody in town and
all over Rocky Ridge is going to be so disappointed."

Jimmy ran a grimy hand through his short black hair.
"Why's that?"

Why? Didn't he understand? "I've talked everyone into
a fever pitch over this ostrich thing, that's why. And now it's
all shot to hell."

Jimmy still looked perplexed. "I don't get it. I mean, I
know you're losing the Red Canyon land, but you've still
got the birds. Why can't you just move 'em and keep going?"

"Yeah, right."

"I'm serious. Stow 'em here for a while—we've got some
empty pastureland. Collect a few more eggs, sell 'em and
put a down payment on a new place. Hey, you know, the
Murphy farm is for sale."

"That's crazy, Jimmy," she said dejectedly. "It'd never
work."

"Me, crazy? You have a lot of room to talk. My idea ain't
no crazier than yours was to begin with. You're being too
sentimental about that land of Clem Shaner's."

"Oh, what do you know about it?"

He shrugged and left her alone with her thoughts.

Was her brother right? she wondered. Zach, too, had
suggested moving the birds, and she'd rejected the idea out
of hand. Maybe she was being hardheaded because she was
more upset over Zach's lack of loyalty to the Red Canyon

and his exit from her life than she was about losing the ranch itself. Otherwise, why was she so sure she couldn't raise birds in another nearby location?

Somehow, her love for Zach had gotten all tied up with the Red Canyon, until she couldn't visualize one without the other. Had she become so attached to the dream of living happily with Zach on Shaner land that she'd become blind to reasonable alternatives?

More significant, had she become so attached to an idealized version of Zach that she couldn't accept him as he really was? Just because he couldn't rub a magic lamp and make all the details work out to her satisfaction, that didn't make him a heartless beast. When he couldn't come up with the money to pay off the bank, he had tried to explore other options. He'd tried to find something to please her. And she had refused to compromise even a little.

Not only that, but she hadn't come up with any schemes of her own to save her dream. She had invested every shred of hope in her heart in Zach's ability to make everything all right. And when he couldn't, she'd turned on him.

Guiltily she recalled the way she'd fled the ranch, gathering up her personal belongings and stuffing them in the back of Jimmy's pickup, leaving not so much as a note of explanation for Zach to find when he returned.

She knew how disappointed he would be to discover her gone. Perhaps she had even deliberately tried to inflict some measure of pain on him, out of some cockeyed notion that he deserved it. But he hadn't hurt her on purpose. He was simply a businessman, making sensible decisions. Her failure to accept that about him was both childish and unfair.

She looked at her watch. There was still time to undo the damage. She could return to the Red Canyon and put everything back before Zach showed up, and he'd be none the wiser—

"Ellie!" her mother's shrill voice called from inside the house. "Ellie, where are you? There's someone here to see you."

Oh, Lord, no! She knew, even before she heard those familiar, measured footsteps heading for the back door, who had come to call. She looked a mess and probably smelled worse after her visit to the hog pen. She frantically tugged off her offending boots and socks, tossing them into a corner of the screened-in porch just as Zach burst from the house.

Every line of his body communicated outrage as he glared at her through slitted green eyes that suddenly looked like those of a cat. A big cat.

Even when she'd hardly known Zach, she had sensed that to anger him would be foolish. Now she understood just how accurate her instincts were. Unconsciously she took a half step backward. "H-hi, Zach."

"Don't 'Hi Zach' me. How dare you?"

"How dare I say hi?"

"How dare you pack up and leave the ranch without telling me? Do you have any idea what it felt like to walk into that house and find you gone and your room empty? Not even a note, for crissakes!"

Ellie had never seen him so angry. His voice was loud enough to raise the roof. Without looking, she knew her mother was peeking through the curtain at the kitchen window, and her father and brother were standing by with their shotguns.

"Well?"

"First off," she said, "I'd suggest you lower your voice, unless you like the idea of tearing out of here with your rump full of buckshot. And second, I can explain." Maybe.

"Oh, really?" his volume was only a notch lower. "I'd like to hear it."

"And I'd like some privacy," she said, casting a wary eye at the curtain fluttering at the kitchen window. "Let's go for

a walk." Without waiting for him to agree, she pushed
through the screen door and headed toward the woods.

He jumped right into step beside her. "Where are your
shoes?"

"I don't need shoes," she said. "I spent most of my
childhood barefoot." She didn't add that her feet were con-
siderably more tender now than they used to be. Small twigs
and pebbles on the path she'd chosen through the trees made
her wince.

When she judged that they'd traveled far enough away
from prying eyes, she stopped and leaned back against a tall
pine tree, trying to compose her thoughts.

Zach stood nearby, arms folded, the toe of one boot tapping with furious impatience.

"Look, I'm sorry, okay?" she said. "It was a lousy thing
to do. I'd already decided to go back—before you got here."

He shot her a dubious look.

"I got too emotional," she tried again, babbling in her
effort to make him understand. "I couldn't stay there. Everything reminded me of—" *Of you.* "Of what I was losing, and I couldn't take it anymore. The ranch means so
much to—"

"Hang the ranch! You have no idea how sick I am of
talking about that miserable little piece of acreage and those
brainless birds. What about us? Or is there no 'us' apart
from the Red Canyon?"

"I . . . I didn't think there was."

"So all this time I've been a means to an end, is that it?
You've been using me, manipulating my emotions to save
your damn ranch."

She shook her head vehemently. "Zach, you know that's
not true."

"I don't know anything anymore." He reached behind
him and pulled out a thick white envelope from the back
pocket of his jeans. "Here," he said, handing her the envelope. "This is what I came to the ranch to tell you about."

"What...what is it?" The sealed envelope shook in her trembling hands.

"Open it and see for yourself."

She broke the seal and pulled out a sheaf of what looked to be legal documents of some sort. Other than her own name, which was on the top of several of the papers, she couldn't make heads or tails of them. Was he filing a lawsuit against her, or what? "I can't decipher these!" she cried in frustration. "What do they mean?"

"They mean that you're now the proud owner of the Red Canyon Ranch, lock, stock and feathers. The bank has withdrawn its demand."

It took a few moments for the full import of his explanation to hit her. "How did you...? But I don't want it," she said, thrusting the papers back at him.

He stared back at her incredulously. "You don't *want* it?" he repeated. "Dammit, woman, I busted my buns to save your damn ranch. I stayed up all night, twisted the arms of my friends, put my personal reputation on the line, not to mention my trust fund, and you tell me you don't *want* it?"

He didn't understand, she realized. But she could hardly blame him for that. The answers were only now starting to sink into her own brain. "The Red Canyon doesn't mean a hill of beans to me unless you come with it," she said softly. "I love you, Zach. I love the ranch, too, but if I have to choose, I'd rather have you. I might even learn to like St. Louis."

Zach simply stared at her, dumbfounded, until slowly the tension seemed to drain out of him and a lazy smile spread across his face. "Now what could possibly attract you to St. Louis?"

"You! Didn't I just say that?"

He shook his head. "I won't be there. I'll be down here. That is, I was hoping you'd let me live at your ranch."

Her heart did a flip-flop that could have registered on the Richter scale. "What exactly are you saying?"

He dropped his teasing facade. "Your plan worked, honey. This land, the mountains, they're in my blood. Even if no one had told me I was born here, I think I would have felt the connection. I want to live here, permanently. I want to raise children here and teach them about what's important in life. I want to...dammit, I want to raise ostriches. And I want a woman by my side, one who knows something about making dreams come true."

It never occurred to Ellie to play coy. She'd nearly blown the whole shootin' match by keeping her feelings inside. No more. "I could do it," she said, nodding eagerly. "I could be that woman."

Zach laughed and pulled her into his arms. "You're the only woman I would even consider for the position," he said just before dropping his head to claim her lips with his.

Ellie's heart beat a wild rhythm as he teased and tantalized. Never had a kiss felt so right, so perfect, as if their souls were intertwined as securely as their bodies. It was only when his hand slipped under her T-shirt to cup her breast that she remembered where she was. "Mmm, Zach, remember what I said about that buckshot? If my brother takes a notion to come looking for me—"

A chuckle rumbled low in Zach's throat. "A shotgun wedding. Perfect. That way we can skip all the planning and worrying.... Ellie, you do understand that I want to marry you, right?"

"As a matter of fact, you, uh, didn't mention it."

"Well, consider it mentioned. Is that okay?"

"Is *that* a proposal?"

"Ellie Kessler, will you marry me?"

She grinned as her dreams for the future expanded and glowed with a life of their own. "On one condition." She waved the envelope at him. "You change these ownership papers so that both our names are on them. That way neither of us will ever be tempted to walk away from the ranch."

"And neither of us can sell it, either. That's a pretty inflexible arrangement."

"Does that bother you? 'Cause if it does—"

"No, silly, it doesn't bother me. I won't change my mind about this, not ever again. That ranch will belong to both of us, come hell or high water."

They sealed the agreement with another wild kiss.

"I declare, I don't know how I ever fit into that dress," Flo said as she fingered the sleeve of the aged satin gown Ellie wore, the same gown in which both Ellie's mother and grandmother had been married.

The floor-length dress, with its long sleeves, high neck and heavy train, was too warm by far for a July wedding, but Ellie wouldn't have dreamed of wearing anything else. For once in her life she felt like a princess, worthy of the prince in the somber gray suit who stood at her side, his hand resting lightly but possessively at her waist.

The small, private church ceremony had taken only a few minutes. But now it was time for the reception, and Ellie was sure everyone within a fifty-mile radius had come to toast the health and success of their two brave bird ranchers. A huge blue-and-white striped tent had been erected in one of the Red Canyon's empty pastures to accommodate the crowd. Bessie Peebles had baked the wedding cake—a little lopsided, but no doubt delicious. Angie Kelso had provided flowers from her garden. Marjean, Betty and Rita, the waitresses from Rosie's Café, were serving up barbecue.

The canvas shielded the guests from the sun, but it was still hot. Perspiration tickled the back of Ellie's neck, and she was sure her face was shiny as a mirror, despite all the powder she'd applied.

A handsome man with curly black hair and tortoiseshell glasses approached the happy couple, his hand extended.

"Jeff!" Zach said. "Glad you could make it."

So, this was the illustrious business partner, the one who was buying out Zach's half of the financial-consulting firm.

Jeff reached out to shake Ellie's hand, and at the last minute kissed it instead. "So, you're Ellie," he said, giving her a once-over. "I don't mind telling you, I think you saved this guy from an ulcer."

"Are you kidding?" Zach objected. "I think she gave me one. But it's all better now," he added quickly when she surreptitiously pinched his behind. "Hey, what happened to your dad, Ellie?"

"He's probably in the barn, visiting his chick. He can't wait till it's big enough to take home."

"He's not the only one in the barn. I think most of our guests are more interested in looking at our stock than eating wedding cake." Zach pulled her to him for a quick kiss. "You're a pretty shrewd businesswoman, Mrs. Shaner, throwing a wedding reception and showing off your birds all at the same time."

"Don't knock it. I'll be selling egg shares and chick shares right and left when this is over."

"*After* the honeymoon," he reminded her.

Ben Poteet came through the reception line next. After kissing the bride and wishing the couple good luck, he put his arm around Zach's shoulders. "Now, about that acre on the southwest corner of my property—"

"*Your* property!" Zach cut in. "If it's yours, how come it's on my side of the fence?"

"Because you uncle was a thief!"

Ellie winked at Jeff, who stared in open-mouthed astonishment, letting him know that everything was as it should be.

"And furthermore," Ben continued, just getting warmed up, "the original survey for that—holy cheese, would ya look at that?" His eyes bulged with astonishment as he nodded toward the opposite end of the tent. A lone ostrich hen was wandering in like she owned the place, casually eyeing the wedding cake. One woman screamed and jumped onto a folding chair. Bessie stood in front of the cake, knife raised, ready to defend it against the intruder.

Before Ellie could even react, Jimmy came running in behind the hen, his coat and tie gone, his shirtsleeves rolled up to the elbow. "Ellie! Zach! Someone opened the gate to the ostrich pasture. The birds are running loose all over the place!"

Ellie looked at her husband. "Well, partner, it was a nice interlude," she said, stepping out of her high heels and looping her train over her arm. "Shall we show these folks how to bird wrangle?"

Zach was already shrugging out of his jacket. "After you."

What followed was worse than any Three Stooges antics Ellie had ever seen. The wedding guests howled and slapped their knees with glee, and children shrieked in delight as the newlyweds provided the post-wedding entertainment by herding the wayward birds back to their home. Ellie discovered that the ostriches were terrified of her wedding veil, so she pulled it off her head and waved it mercilessly at any who thought to escape. Eventually all eight birds were secured.

"Now who do you suppose opened that gate?" Ellie asked as she brushed a little dust off her gown. She, Zach and Jimmy all looked a little worse for wear as they made their way back to the tent, but thankfully there was no real damage.

"Kids, probably," said Zach.

"Nuh-uh," Jimmy said. "I saw this lady lurking around a few minutes before the birds got loose. Dark hair, lots of makeup."

Zach and Ellie exchanged glances. "Phyllis Quincy," they said at the same time. Apparently their nemesis had decided to perpetrate one final act of malice. The fact that she had resorted to such a silly prank indicated how powerless she really was.

"The lady from SunnyLand?" Jimmy asked. "Hey, I heard SunnyLand made an offer on the Murphy farm."

Ellie sighed. She supposed nothing would stand in the way of the Choctaw Indian Park. Rocky Ridge was just a disorganized little community, after all, and SunnyLand was a huge corporation.

"Hey, don't worry," Jimmy said. "The Murphys turned 'em down flat. I heard they're thinking about selling off their cattle and switching to ostriches. Mr. Murphy said after he saw how well y'all are doing, he'd be crazy not to give it a try."

Abruptly Ellie's mood lifted. She beamed, first at Jimmy, then at Zach.

Zach grinned back. "Looks like dreams really do come true," he said, looping his arm around his wife's shoulders.

She stood on tiptoe and kissed his cheek, her heart full to overflowing. "I'd still be dreaming if you hadn't come along."

* * * * *

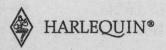
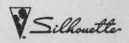

He staked his claim...

HONOR BOUND

by
New York Times
Bestselling Author

As Aislinn Andrews opened her mouth to scream, a hard hand clamped over her face and she found herself face-to-face with Lucas Greywolf, a lean, lethal-looking Navajo and escaped convict who swore he wouldn't hurt her— *if* she helped him.

Look for HONOR BOUND at your favorite retail outlet this January.

Only from...

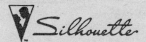

where passion lives.

SILHOUETTE.... Where Passion Lives

Don't miss these Silhouette favorites by some of our most popular authors!
And now, you can receive a discount by ordering two or more titles!

Silhouette Desire®

#05751	THE MAN WITH THE MIDNIGHT EYES BJ James	$2.89	☐
#05763	THE COWBOY Cait London	$2.89	☐
#05774	TENNESSEE WALTZ Jackie Merritt	$2.89	☐
#05779	THE RANCHER AND THE RUNAWAY BRIDE Joan Johnston	$2.89	☐

Silhouette Intimate Moments®

#07417	WOLF AND THE ANGEL Kathleen Creighton	$3.29	☐
#07480	DIAMOND WILLOW Kathleen Eagle	$3.39	☐
#07486	MEMORIES OF LAURA Marilyn Pappano	$3.39	☐
#07493	QUINN EISLEY'S WAR Patricia Gardner Evans	$3.39	☐

Silhouette Shadows®

#27003	STRANGER IN THE MIST Lee Karr	$3.50	☐
#27007	FLASHBACK Terri Herrington	$3.50	☐
#27009	BREAK THE NIGHT Anne Stuart	$3.50	☐
#27012	DARK ENCHANTMENT Jane Toombs	$3.50	☐

Silhouette Special Edition®

#09754	THERE AND NOW Linda Lael Miller	$3.39	☐
#09770	FATHER: UNKNOWN Andrea Edwards	$3.39	☐
#09791	THE CAT THAT LIVED ON PARK AVENUE Tracy Sinclair	$3.39	☐
#09811	HE'S THE RICH BOY Lisa Jackson	$3.39	☐

Silhouette Romance®

#08893	LETTERS FROM HOME Toni Collins	$2.69	☐
#08915	NEW YEAR'S BABY Stella Bagwell	$2.69	☐
#08927	THE PURSUIT OF HAPPINESS Anne Peters	$2.69	☐
#08952	INSTANT FATHER Lucy Gordon	$2.75	☐

	AMOUNT	$
DEDUCT:	10% DISCOUNT FOR 2+ BOOKS	$
	POSTAGE & HANDLING	$
	($1.00 for one book, 50¢ for each additional)	
	APPLICABLE TAXES*	$
	TOTAL PAYABLE	$
	(check or money order—please do not send cash)	

To order, complete this form and send it, along with a check or money order for the total above, payable to Silhouette Books, to: *In the U.S.*: 3010 Walden Avenue, P.O. Box 9077, Buffalo, NY 14269-9077; *In Canada*: P.O. Box 636, Fort Erie, Ontario, L2A 5X3.

Name: _____

Address: _____ City: _____

State/Prov.: _____ Zip/Postal Code: _____

*New York residents remit applicable sales taxes.
Canadian residents remit applicable GST and provincial taxes.

SBACK-OD

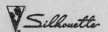